"Get out of the truck! Now!" Stone shouted.

Emily's heart leaped into her throat as she shoved open the truck door. The hood exploded sky-high and a rush of heat thrust her into the air and onto the ground with a thud. Ears ringing, dazed and disoriented, she curled up, hoping to protect herself from the debris raining down on her.

Someone had planted a bomb in Stone's truck.

A second blast shot flames above the trees, and the rest of the truck went up in smoke. Scrambling for the large tree to take cover, Emily scoured the area for any sign of Stone.

How did anyone know she was here? Had her attacker last night followed her? Thoughts zinged through her mind like bullets from a machine gun. She coughed and sputtered, the smoke black and thick like smog.

The house hadn't been touched and she thanked God for that. Emily would never have forgiven herself if Stone's mother or brother had been endangered.

But where was Stone?

Jessica R. Patch lives in the Mid-South, where she pens inspirational contemporary romance and romantic suspense novels. When she's not hunched over her laptop or going on adventurous trips with willing friends in the name of research, you can find her watching way too much Netflix with her family and collecting recipes for amazing dishes she'll probably never cook. To learn more about Jessica, please visit her at jessicarpatch.com.

CRIME SCENE CONSPIRACY

JESSICA R. PATCH

LOVE INSPIRED SUSPENSE
INSPIRATIONAL ROMANCE

LOVE INSPIRED® SUSPENSE
INSPIRATIONAL ROMANCE

Recycling programs
for this product may
not exist in your area.

ISBN-13: 978-1-335-59913-1

Crime Scene Conspiracy

Love Inspired
22 Adelaide St. West, 41st Floor
Toronto, Ontario M5H 4E3, Canada
www.LoveInspired.com

Printed in U.S.A.

Come unto me, all ye that labour and are heavy laden,
and I will give you rest.
—*Matthew* 11:28

For everyone who thinks they must carry a burden alone.

Special thanks:

To my agent, Rachel Kent; my editor, Shana Asaro;
Susan L. Tuttle and Jodie Bailey: Thank you for all you do
to help the books be even better. I treasure each one of you.

ONE

Texas Ranger Emily O'Connell glanced at the old-money mansion, then the white commercial van parked in front and inwardly groaned. How was she going to get past Stone Spencer? His aftermath recovery and trauma services van might as well have been a blaring beacon declaring the horrific event that had recently happened inside, and the week before Christmas. She'd hoped to beat him to the punch and avoid him and the million questions he was no doubt going to ask.

Ignoring the cluster of media vans, hordes of journalists and camera crews filming the home, she focused on the house. Windows facing the circular drive were decked with evergreen wreaths and dotted in the center with red velvet bows. Windowsills were adorned with white taper candles. Probably battery-operated ones that would automatically kick on at sunset. Classic Christmas decor.

Only hours ago, socialite Tiffany Williford

had ended her life by suicide. Holidays were, sadly, one of the highest times of the year for suicides.

But Emily wasn't so sure it had been a suicide at all, and that's why she was here.

Tiffany's much older husband, the Honorable Charles Williford—known by friends as Judge—had found her at eight this morning in her private salon. Emily had passed the CSI vehicles on the long stretch of road leaving the home. With the Cedar Springs PD gone and the forensics processed, it was now up to the Spencer Aftermath Recovery Team to clean it up, but Emily wanted a peek at the crime scene before the process began. Leave it to Stone to be prompt.

Emily had firsthand experience with his timeliness when one of her cases in the Public Integrity Unit had intersected with his, back when he'd also been a Texas Ranger in the Unsolved Homicide Unit. The man was organized, efficient, tough at times but kind, and had a nose like a bloodhound when it came to sniffing out criminals. He'd been sorely missed when he'd resigned his position a few years ago.

He'd also asked her out twice to dinner.

And twice she'd declined.

Glancing in the rearview mirror, she tucked one of her long bangs that had come out of her low bun back where it belonged, then frowned at her freckles. She didn't mind being a redhead. She detested the freckles that covered her body, but she refused to use makeup or concealer to hide them. They were simply her.

Donning her extra wide sunglasses, she reached for her white cattleman hat from the passenger seat out of habit, but it was empty. Today she was in her own vehicle and plain clothes so as not to alert the reporters at the house that a Texas Ranger from the PIU was on the scene. Her Texas star badge was inside her jeans pocket. This was a covert mission.

She exited the vehicle to a balmy sixty-four degrees. Per usual, it didn't look like snow for the Texas Hill Country this Christmas, but anything could happen in a week. A myriad of reporters demanded her identity, but she kept her head down to avoid being caught on camera, being sure not to act too inconspicuous. Her cowgirl boots clicked along the asphalt as she approached the front door. She ignored the reporters' questions and kept her back to the hungry cameras.

Cedar Springs PD might be calling this a suicide—and maybe it was—and the autopsy report might read the same, but she and her director, George Baldwin, needed to know for sure. Judge Williford had ties to Governor Paul Henderson.

And Paul Henderson was why she was here. No one could know. Not yet.

Not even Stone Spencer.

Emily wasn't going to lie—she did work in the Public Integrity Unit after all—but she also wasn't going to share confidential information with the judge or anyone else. Her father used to say one only had their good word. Once that was broken, one could kiss integrity goodbye. Emily had adhered to that philosophy her entire life. It's why she chose the PIU. She and three other Texas Rangers worked full time on cases against public officials and state employees.

Too bad Dad hadn't lived up to his own good counsel.

But her maternal grandfather had. He'd been a Texas Ranger too. Emily only wished he had been alive to see her own silver star.

She rang the doorbell, her spiel on the tip of her tongue. A woman in a uniform opened the door, and the scent of holiday candles and cinnamon wafted toward her.

"No reporters!" the woman barked. "You've been warned already."

Emily fished out her Texas Ranger star and discreetly held it out. "Is the judge home? I'd like to talk to him about his wife."

The housekeeper eyed her attire, or lack of. No light-colored cattleman, no white dress shirt with a crossover tie, black blazer and khaki pants. "I'm trying to be discreet for the judge's sake."

Nodding, the petite woman allowed Emily inside. "He's here. In his study. Hasn't come out to even eat a sandwich for lunch."

Emily glanced at her watch. It was nearing one o'clock. She scanned the pristine home. The marble flooring gleamed, a shiny mahogany banister lined a spiral staircase, an ostentatious foyer chandelier glittered over an equally ostentatious Christmas tree. She skimmed the premises for any sign of Stone or his brothers, who worked with him in the family business. Thankfully, she saw no one.

The housekeeper knocked on a door. "Your Honor, Texas Ranger…" She looked at Emily.

"Emily O'Connell."

"Emily O'Connell from…"

"The Public Integrity Unit," she offered.

She repeated Emily's words. "She's here to talk with you."

Emily heard stirring behind the door, and then it opened to the Honorable Charles Williford. His hair was thick and white, matching his tidy full mustache. He had a Sam Elliott vibe going for him. When he spoke, he sounded like the famous actor too. "Why is the Integrity Unit here?" He eyeballed Emily and her lack of uniform.

"I didn't wear my uniform for discretion." She

held up her badge. "You can call my supervisor if you'd like. I'm not a reporter trying to be sneaky."

"It was…suicide," he said, choking on his words. His dark eyes were bloodshot, and the room smelled of pipe tobacco and grief.

"Yes, Your Honor, I heard." She laid a hand on his bicep, feeling his pain in her chest. "I'm so sorry for your loss. I'm just here to do my job. I'll make it quick and then leave you."

"Did someone report foul play?" He sighed. "I don't understand why you'd be here otherwise."

They hadn't been tipped off about *this* particular incident; there'd been no formal complaint or evidence. But a Texas Ranger who had been assigned protective duty to the governor had come to George Baldwin two weeks ago with allegations, several photos he'd pulled from the iCloud, and his written and recorded statement saying he believed Governor Paul Henderson had directly murdered or indirectly had three women killed in the past four years.

All three women had been related to men who were fraternity brothers with Paul Henderson, and all three women had been in the governor's presence within days of their deaths.

Tiffany Williford brought the count up to four.

Granted, the photos had only proved the women had been in contact with the governor, but according to Ranger Gil McElroy, their deaths had not been suicides or accidents. The man's word was strong, but there was no proof. But a week after Ranger McElroy came to see George in the PIU, he too died by an accident.

Emily didn't believe that was any accident. So she was in the preliminary stage of investigating. Gathering information that would substantiate Ranger McElroy's allegation or refute it.

"We both know I'm not at liberty to say, sir."

His eyebrow raised at her vagueness, but he nodded and allowed her inside his study. This wasn't exactly normal protocol, but the scope of this mission was highly confidential. Lives were at stake. Possibly even Emily's and her supervisor's.

Four women were now dead and one Texas Ranger.

If it turned out that the governor was responsible, then it meant he had a string of important and powerful people on his payroll, like law enforcement and even the ME's office. Who knew how far and wide it reached. No one could be trusted.

"Can you answer a few questions for me? I'm sure you've already answered them for the local detectives."

"Sure. Have a seat." He swept his hand out for her to sit in one of the burgundy leather chairs in front of his desk.

Emily retrieved a notepad and pen from her purse. "When was the last time you saw your wife?"

"Two days ago. I was at a speaking engagement in Dallas that ended yesterday afternoon. I had planned to stay on and fly in later today in order to visit with a few old friends, but I changed my mind and got an earlier flight, which put me home a little before eight this morning."

"Anyone know you were coming home early?" she asked and jotted a few notes.

"No. I was going to surprise Tiff and take her to brunch."

"Anyone know about you leaving?"

"Of course. Friends. Family. Colleagues."

She'd verify the travel information. She'd thought her own father was the epitome of integrity, but three months ago when he passed away, she discovered he'd lived a double life complete with a whole new family in Oklahoma, which included a daughter and son only a few years younger than Emily. Her entire life and her mom's entire married life, and they'd never known it. How stupid were they?

"What did you do when you returned home?"

"I came in, looked at the mail and poured a glass of OJ then went into Tiffany's dressing room and bathroom. I found her…on the floor…" He shook his head. "I have no idea why she'd do this. Didn't seem real. I even mentioned to Detective Lang, the lead from Cedar Springs, that this might be a homicide, though there was no forced entry. I looked myself."

Sometimes the signs of suicidal tendencies weren't obvious. And in this case, there may not have been any signs. Not if it was a homicide. She'd know more once she saw the scene—if Stone hadn't already cleaned it up. Even the judge thought it might be foul play.

Women didn't typically use their husbands' guns to end their lives. They took pills and drank them down with alcohol or sat in a running car in a garage. Even jumped. But guns were not on the top of the list, and Tiffany Williford didn't seem the type to do it that way. Once they'd heard that she had supposedly killed herself with one shot to the head, Emily and George had been suspicious. Not to mention Tiffany had recently been at a Christmas charity event with the governor, and she'd had a meeting with him only days before her death.

"Can I see the salon?" A fancy word for a big bathroom. Emily's bath had one vanity, one toilet and a cracker box standup shower with no tub.

"Of course. Marlene will show you." He pressed a button on his phone, and a few moments later, the housekeeper arrived, a sandwich in hand.

"You must eat, Judge. Even half. Please."

He sighed and motioned for her to put the plate on his desk. "Thank you. I'll… I'll try."

Emily followed Marlene up the winding staircase to the west wing of the home.

"This is the primary bedroom, and her private salon is through there, but we've been asked to stay out so the company can…clean." Marlene's chin wobbled and she shook her head.

Emily heard voices from inside the bedroom, a mix of male timbres, and recognized the deep, rich, commanding voice of Stone Spencer himself. Her stomach dipped against her will, and she stepped across the threshold into the bedroom, noticing another Christmas tree in blush pink, white and silver by the bedside. The soft white lights still glowed.

Stone's two brothers stood near the foot of the bed in white hazmat suits, but without head gear, which meant they hadn't begun the cleaning process. Both were over six feet. One had jet-black hair and eyes to match—and a cocky grin that wasn't going to win him any points from her. The other brother had lighter brown hair and eyes, and he wore no smile.

Where was Stone?

"I think you may be lost," the brother with midnight hair said, his tone buttery.

"Doubtful," she said.

Stone stepped into the door frame of the

salon—hazmat suit and a scowl pulling his eyebrows together. Stone was the best looking of the three, in her opinion, and probably the most irritated at being interrupted. At first, he didn't seem to recognize her, then it hit him and his sharp green eyes narrowed. "Emily? Out!" He pointed for her to exit the way she entered.

"Hello, Stone. Nice to see you too. Crime's not in here and the scene's been processed. I think I'll stay. But I appreciate you commanding me like a dog."

He huffed. "Sorry, it's just... Why are you here? This is a suicide." But his eyes betrayed him. He didn't buy that. He pointed to the hallway. "Can we speak in private please?" he asked and waited while she acquiesced. He wasn't usually this abrupt, but it was clear something was flustering him. She ventured into the hall with him, the smell of chemicals and gunpowder still lingering on the air. "I'm sorry for the barking. It's just... I'll get you some protective wear so you don't step in anything."

Guess it wasn't pretty.

Death never was.

Stone Spencer clomped down the spiral staircase and out to his van, where he retrieved a spare hazmat suit, bristling at the media gawking and cawing like ravens ready to pick at a meal. It wasn't that long ago they were outside his family ranch, filming and asking about his own sister's suicide.

Four years had passed but the ache felt like yesterday. Stone hadn't seen a single sign, and he'd borne that guilt every hour of the day since. He felt it even more today. Every suicide brought back the grief from Paisley's death. Mom had never been the same, especially since they'd lost his father to a heart attack six months prior to Pai's death.

But right now, Stone didn't have time to think about his pain or his mom's vacant eyes when she'd asked who would clean up the aftermath Paisley had left behind. That's when Stone had recognized a great need among families. He'd resigned from the Texas Rangers and moved back to their ailing family ranch to start his aftermath recovery company. His sister Sissy, a therapist, had joined to handle the grief counseling services they offered. There was always more than physical aftermath to a tragedy.

Rhode, his youngest brother, had joined the team out of no choice, and Bridge, only two years younger than Stone, had never given a reason for leaving the FBI and coming on board. Stone had never asked. Everyone had their private motives.

The media hounding him reminded him that

everyone felt entitled to information that was none of their business. He ignored their cameras and questions and returned upstairs to Emily.

She was a striking woman with fiery hair that matched her spicy personality. He admired her moxie—not many women became Texas Rangers, which was a shame, but her hard work and shattering of glass ceilings were quite admirable to Stone. While working a case together, he'd asked her to dinner, and she'd turned him down. When the case was finished, he asked again, assuming she didn't date coworkers and that was the reason behind her previous rejection. But she turned him down again. He never figured out why. After all, who said no to tacos and guac? He wasn't a stalker, so he let bygones be bygones, then Pai died.

He handed Emily the hazmat suit. "Here. Just slip it on over your clothes, which by the way, why aren't you in uniform?" She was dressed casual in jeans, a pretty shirt and cowboy boots. She looked Texan through and through, and he had a sudden urge to try one more time for the tacos.

Instead he waited on her answer.

She slipped into the hazmat suit and turned up her nose. She might not think it the most flattering attire, but she looked good to him.

His brothers had already brought up the industrial supplies and biohazard waste container. They cast a few glances his way, but he ignored them too.

"So why aren't you in uniform?" he asked again.

"I'm here in a less formal capacity," she said in a no-nonsense tone. "May I see the scene now? I'm asking out of courtesy."

He was well aware she had authority here as a Texas Ranger and he was a civilian. Some days he missed his job, but he didn't regret his present occupation. He still helped people.

Stone pointed to the bath and dressing room. Emily strode across the white carpet, glanced toward his brothers, and then she entered.

Her lips pursed as she surveyed the vanity littered with cosmetics, perfumes and lotions. The stool had been knocked over, and blood spatter dotted the floor and the garden tub behind her. The spatter was consistent with someone shooting themselves in the forehead, but something felt off to him.

Emily studied the spatter on the floor, the way the blood pooled. "You see the body before they took her?"

"No. We aren't allowed in until after the CSI is finished and the victim's taken and the scene is released. Do you not have access to the crime scene photos?"

Her jaw twitched, and she stood in front of the vanity, then squatted as if she were sitting on the toppled stool, staring into the mirror. The array of LED lights lit up the freckles rolling over her nose and cheeks, providing her a younger appearance than her midthirties. Soft brown eyes met his and his gut felt like it'd been punched.

"She shot herself right between the eyes while sitting on that stool," she said, waiting on him to respond.

He'd heard that was the case, but it didn't feel right. Blood spatter often told the tale, and in this case, while there was spatter, it didn't seem there was enough of it on the bathtub and wall behind it, and there wasn't as much on the floor as he'd expected. If he had to make a conclusion, he'd say that she was shot after she died but before livor mortis began, which was a tight window of twenty to thirty minutes. He'd be interested in the photos of the victim. If she shot herself, there would be blowback on her hands and a specific pattern. He wondered if Emily had seen the photos or got some kind of tip, and that's why she was here to investigate.

"Did you get a tip that Judge killed his wife? Why else would you be here?" he asked.

"I'm not at liberty to say why I'm here, Stone, and you know how irritating it is when people ignore that statement. So maybe let me think for half a second." She huffed and took a few photos with her cell phone camera.

It was irritating when the tables were turned. "I'll give you space, but I can keep confidences."

"Bully for you," she muttered, and instead of frustrating him, he found her amusing.

He'd offer her an olive branch. "We don't think this was a suicide, Emily." He explained why and pointed out the blood spatter patterns on the floor and tub and tiled wall behind the tub.

Finally she glared at him. "You talk well and a lot. But you listen terribly and too little."

He held up his hands. He was supposed to be giving her space. Slowly, holding in his smirk, he backed out of the bathroom and gave her room to assess the situation herself. She was fully capable and fully feisty, the kind of woman who gave a man heartburn he didn't want or need.

Finally, she exited the bathroom. His brothers, who had been wondering why she was here and who she was, moseyed into the hall, giving them privacy. They'd hit him up after for the scoop.

"Well?" he asked.

Emily graced him with a resolute nod. "Well, thank you for the privacy. It was good to see you, Stone. The work you're doing is good. I'll see myself out." She marched past him, leaving him gawking at an empty room.

That was it? No answers? No thoughts or theories? He'd given her an olive branch!

"Gentlemen," she said in the hall, and then his brothers reentered the room.

"She's fun," Rhode said with a smug grin.

Bridge elbowed Rhode. "I don't know about fun," he said as he pointed to Stone, "but your face matches her hair."

"It's a good color on you, bro," Rhode added and laughed as he pulled on his headgear.

Stone didn't have time to race after her. Besides, she was doing her job, but it rankled him for the entire two hours it took to clean up the aftermath of Tiffany Williford's death. By the time they finished, no one would know that only hours ago, a life was lost in a brutal way and that people were grieving her. The cleanup gave loved ones relief, but it never cleaned up the brokenness.

The Spencer family could attest to that.

Stone glanced at his GPS monitor. Emily O'Connell lived about thirty miles outside Austin in a little town called Golden Creek. His GPS had him going straight down the main street of the historical downtown. It reminded him of those small towns in the romantic movies his sister Sissy used to watch before she was widowed. At ten o'clock it was late to be paying an unannounced visit, but Tiffany Williford's manner of death wouldn't give Stone any peace. The past four years he'd done this job had practically turned him into a forensic expert in blood spatter.

Something wasn't adding up.

He'd called his cousin, Detective Dom DeMarco, in Cedar Springs and talked with him, but he wasn't on the case. Detective Neil Lang was the lead. Dom had gone to pull the photos to see if Stone's hunch was right, but the photos hadn't been in the case files. Dom said he'd look into it. But the ME had ruled it suicide. It was done. He'd told Stone to move on. He wasn't an investigator anymore. That was true. He wasn't. He had zero authority to run off on a gut instinct.

But Emily had shown up at the Williford house, and she might have seen the photos prior to them vanishing. Was she investigating Judge? He had been a longtime family friend. They'd even known his first wife before she passed of cancer eight years ago. Stone's father had gone to college on a scholarship and worked his behind off for everything he had, but his fraternity brothers were old money and had become powerful people. Many had offered to help with his ranch debts that occurred when he'd gotten sick, but Dad was a prideful man and wouldn't take the handout. He'd dug himself out of debt and held on to the ranch by a thread. It was still hanging by a thread.

Why was Emily at the scene if not in conjunction with Judge? When she'd walked out of that bathroom, she'd been stoic, but he'd caught the truth for a moment in her eyes. She'd seen what Stone had seen.

The sloppy cover-up.

Surely it wasn't at Judge's hands.

The GPS announced his arrival on the right. He parked behind a white car with government tags. Probably Emily's. A string of shops, boutiques and restaurants lined the sleepy street. At her address, the storefront quilt shop was dark, but the window on the third floor glowed with colored Christmas lights. He guessed Emily lived in an apartment above the business.

Stone clambered out and strode between the narrow alley connecting the quilt shop to a candle store. The air was stilted and dry. Around back was a black iron staircase spiraling up to the third floor. How did she make this climb every day? He imagined her legs were a lovely product of the daily workout. Stone began the ascent, his boots clicking quietly against the iron, until he reached the small stoop with a modest herb garden and a pair of rubber boots by the door. He raised his knuckles to knock but noticed the door was cracked open.

A shriek rang out and the sound of heavy furniture crashing sent his heart into a skitter.

He pulled his gun and barged into Emily's home.

Glass shattered.

A gun fired.

TWO

Emily's breath came in pants as the attacker charged her again, unafraid of the bullet she'd discharged. It had landed in the wall next to his head. The dark-clad figure launched himself at her, knocking her to the hall floor. She lost her grip on the gun, and it skittered across the hardwood and under the Christmas tree in the living room.

She'd been in bed reading when she thought she heard a noise, and her security cam app notified her of movement. As she'd entered the dark kitchen, the intruder had made his move.

He straddled her and wrapped his gloved hands around her throat. She smelled hints of cigarette smoke and body odor. His position made it impossible to bring her knee up and clobber his tender spot. Her lungs burned and pressure built in her head. She bucked and thrashed, hoping to throw him off, when she heard a gritty voice call her name.

Stone! Stone Spencer was in her house.

The intruder heard it too. He froze, snapped his head toward the living room, then coldcocked her. Patches of darkness weaved before her eyes as her head spun, but his weight lifted, and he darted into her bedroom. Dazed, she lay still but the room spun.

Then Stone was at her side. "Emily! Hey!"

"I'm o…kay…" She pointed behind her, and Stone wasted no time, eating up the hallway floor to the bedroom. Emily rubbed her jaw and forced herself into a sitting position, her heart thundering against her ribs. Working her way to her feet, she swayed and grabbed the wall to steady herself.

Stone returned, his strong hand on her upper arm. "Take it easy, killer," he said and guided her into the living room and to her couch. "Just sit down. He went down the fire escape. He's gone."

Emily moaned and leaned her head against the couch, closing her eyes and breathing deeply as a bout of nausea swept through her. Stone's fingers grazed her swelling cheek, his thumb soft, but oh so masculine against her jawline.

"He got you good." He whistled low and she opened her eyes and caught him surveying her cozy living room and small open dining area between the living room and kitchen. "Did he ransack the place? You walk in on a burglary?"

"No. That's from the struggle."

Pieces of the broken vases and lamps she'd hurled at her attacker littered the floor. Chairs, books and Christmas presents were askew, and the star on top of her tree was tilted to the right. She wasn't going to go down without a fight.

"Remind me to never get into it with you."

She had a feeling battling it out with Stone would produce more than some overturned furniture. "Can I hire you for your aftermath services? I *so* don't want to clean this up." She smiled and winced.

Stone chuckled. "Nice to see you still have your sense of humor." He left her on the couch, then she heard the freezer door open and close, then drawers. He entered with an ice pack and a hand towel that read, *Burned in Love*. He held it up. "Is this a declaration of the state of your heart or that you can't cook?"

Both.

"Ha. Ha," she said instead and accepted the ice pack.

He returned to the kitchen, then came back with a bottle of pain relievers and a glass of water. "You're tough. You can make it go down without sugar." He handed her the glass and emptied two pills into her palm.

Once she had the meds down and the ice pack

on her jaw, she tried to relax, but her insides were like a frantic rat in a maze unable to find the exit.

"You want to tell me what happened, or are you still not at liberty to say?" he asked her.

"Why are you here? To hear that again?" She waved off the words. "Sorry. I'm actually glad you're in my apartment like a bullheaded pig demanding I tell you the details of my case. I mean, I don't plan on doing that, but the fact that you intervened is helpful." She dropped her ice pack and sighed. "You really live up to your name. Hardheaded like a rock."

"You need to work on your thank-yous." His eyebrows inched north, then his lips swiveled to the side. He sat beside her, the faint scent of a spicy cologne reaching her nostrils and signaling a flutter in her belly. "Tell me this break-in was a burglary gone wrong and has nothing to do with why you were at the Williford mansion, and I'll make sure the door can be locked and I'll leave. I noticed it had been tampered with. You're a strong capable woman who can multitask. Not many people can fend off an intruder while trashing their living room so expertly." He turned serious. "Can you tell me that?"

She wished she could, but with the nature of the case, she was almost certain that whoever had entered her apartment was there to kill her, not swipe a TV. She didn't lie, so she wouldn't now.

"I can't say that."

"What can you say?" he asked calmly. "And maybe try not to be *wily* about it," he drawled slowly and, oh, so cowboy-like.

She'd watched the news all evening, and while a couple of networks had filmed her going inside the Williford house, with her sunglasses and head down, she'd been hard to identify. But if someone knew her well, she supposed they'd recognize her.

Maybe she was being watched. Maybe everyone in the PIU since Ranger McElroy had shown up in George's office was being watched. Maybe McElroy had been followed. Emily's discretion hadn't paid off. Someone knew she was digging.

She gazed up at Stone. His sandy brown hair had likely once been blond as a child, and it was a little longer than when he was a Texas Ranger. His green eyes, framed by even darker lashes, held a menacing appearance without meaning to. Elementary school teachers had probably made him sit up front automatically. A Greek nose and full lips made him a fine specimen, but his dimples, like glorious pools set in his scruffy cheeks, only added to his bad-boy appeal. But Stone Spencer was no bad boy. And it wasn't his looks drawing her to him at the moment. It was steel in his eyes and the concern pulsing within them.

"You can trust me, O'Connell."

Oh, how she wanted to believe that. She'd thought about it after leaving the Williford mansion earlier today. If the four women who had died within the past four years had actually been murdered, that meant the first victim would have been Stone's eldest sister, Paisley Spencer.

Paul Henderson had been a family friend since the frat days with Stone's father. There was a measure of loyalty there to Governor Henderson. However, Stone would surely be an ally to Emily if he believed that Paul had a hand in his sister's death and cover-up. Wouldn't he?

And would he believe Emily? Could he believe that a man he'd known his whole life was a killer? If he didn't believe it, he might not be an ally to her.

She'd been all up in her head since seeing Stone on the scene. Her job wasn't an easy one. She saw the underbelly of humanity—the greed, corruption and deceit. Then her father's betrayal. She'd trusted him. Thought he'd hung the moon.

She'd been wrong. Duped. Lied to.

Never again.

Even if she thought she could trust Stone, that he'd believe her, her stomach ached at the idea of having to reveal the awful truth.

His sister had likely been murdered.

But she was in trouble. Powerful people had

deep pockets and wide reaches. If they wanted Emily dead, she'd end up dead. However, she wasn't going to let go of this case. Women were dying, and officials of the highest order might be pulling the strings. Corruption abounded and laws were being broken. Not only was it her job, she had a compelling need to make wrong things right. That alone would keep up her stamina and strength.

"I don't trust anyone, Spencer," she finally said, using his last name—a way to show camaraderie and friendship among Texas Rangers. "Even if I did completely trust you, I'd be putting you in grave danger. Maybe even your family. I won't have that on my head."

Stone leaned in and laid his strong hand on her shaky one, tightening his grip. "I'm not asking you to take the responsibility of my safety— or my family's. I'll carry it myself. But my gut says something big is going on, and I want to help you. Please let me help you, Emily. Not because I don't think you can take care of yourself or that you're a woman, but Texas Rangers have each other's backs. They stick together. I may not be one officially, but I'm still one here." He pointed to his heart. "I'm for you and I'm with you. You *can* trust me."

Those words were powerful and comforting even if she continued to harbor doubt. She needed a shoulder to lean on, eyes on her back and a partner at her side. Stone was offering, and it could be to her advantage. Since he was out of the game, no one would suspect him of snooping or investigating.

But the fact that the Spencer family had ties to the governor and his family niggled at her. What if she was making a mistake?

The disaster surrounding her and her still-aching throat and face won the battle.

"What I'm about to tell you is only known by one other person—George Baldwin, my director. What I know has already gotten one man killed—a Texas Ranger named Gil McElroy."

"I thought he died in a car accident last week. I attended the funeral Thursday."

Emily hadn't seen him there, but it had been packed. "We don't believe it was accidental. We believe it was staged, and we believe three other women's deaths, and now Tiffany's, were staged too." This was going to be tough to reveal, and she hated to be the one to bear the horrifying news, but if Stone was going to be a part of this, then he had to know the whole truth. She laid a gentle hand on his arm. "Stone, what I'm about to reveal is going to be a gut punch. Okay?"

He gave one resolute nod.

"I believe Paisley's death is possibly the first

of a string of staged suicides or accidents at the hands or command of Governor Paul Henderson."

Stone gawked, then he collapsed against the couch, dazed. She understood the impact of those words. She'd felt it not long ago herself and was still processing. She quietly let the news seep in as he worked through the revelation, his expression morphing from shock to anger as his nostrils flared and his jaw twitched.

"How do you know this? What evidence do you have?" he asked quietly.

Emily removed the ice pack from her face. "Gil came to us two weeks ago because he'd spent the past four years on protection detail for Governor Henderson. He'd been wrestling and he had no proof, but a year ago at an event at the Governor's mansion, Henderson and a woman named Deidre Dillion—"

"That's our mayor's niece. My sister Paisley was friends with her."

Emily nodded. "She was having an affair with the governor, Stone. That can be proven by people—Gil and other Texas Rangers who covered his security detail. I mean, everyone knows the governor is a womanizer. Even his own wife and kids. But that night, he and Deidre got into a serious argument that turned physical. Gil broke it up and heard Henderson threaten her. She left the party, and Henderson went into his office alone. The next morning, the news broke—"

"She accidentally drowned in a hotel Jacuzzi in Austin. She'd been on drugs." Stone leaned forward, his elbows on his knees. "I thought that was odd, because her mother was a recovering drug addict, and she was a huge advocate for drug prevention. She and Paisley talked about that a lot. So, it's not true?"

"Not that it was accidental. I can't request the autopsy photos, or I'll give away what I suspect. We think Henderson has the ME and some law enforcement officials covering up and fudging records."

"So, even if you did request the autopsy report, without seeing the body or being present during the autopsy, you won't know for sure."

"Exactly. The report said she'd taken quite a few Xanax, but Gil said she came to the party and went straight upstairs. Was there less than thirty minutes. It got ugly. She left and appeared to have all her faculties, not even a slight stumble."

"If Gil knew this, then why did he wait until two weeks ago to say anything?"

Emily had asked the same questions. "He had no proof. So he spent time researching. Besides his own eye witness accounts, what he had was flimsy. I'm doing a quiet investigation to see if I can find more substantial evidence."

But it was tricky since she had to be quiet about it, and no one could be trusted.

"The photos of Tiffany Williford that my detective cousin at Cedar Springs PD couldn't find. You think he will?"

Emily shook her head. "No. I think they've been lost or misplaced on purpose. Meaning someone is on the take. Maybe this lead detective Neil Lang."

Stone rubbed his temples. "How does Paisley's death fit?"

"It follows the pattern Gil gave us. Tragedies and suicides among women who had ties to the governor directly or indirectly. One is Lexi Bryant two years ago. Her dad is a businessman and fraternity brother of the governor. By the way, the mayor was also in Paul Henderson's college fraternity—"

"So was my dad. And Paisley is dead." Stone jumped to his feet and began to pace. "I knew something was off. She wouldn't slit her wrists—wouldn't kill herself. I mean, she'd been a bit agitated prior to her death, but I thought it had to do with PJ dumping her."

The governor's son. Only his inner circle called him PJ. To the public, he was Paul Junior.

"You might be too close to this." Bringing Stone in on this might have been a bad idea.

Stone froze. "I'm not. I have to find out if Paul

Henderson killed or had my sister killed and staged her death. You have to let me in, Emily. If you don't, I'll run with it myself."

She was afraid of that.

"And we still have to discuss where you're going to stay now," he added. "This is way bigger than you can handle alone. You need someone on your six. Pack a bag. You're coming with me."

"Now hold up!" She stood and wobbled. He helped to right her.

"Sorry. Sorry. I don't mean to go all caveman. Please come back to the ranch with me. It's off the beaten path and I can keep you safe."

"Yeah, well, who's gonna keep you safe?" She didn't want to leave her house, but Stone had a point. It was only a matter of time before another attempt on her life was made. She might be better off in Cedar Springs on a ranch in the middle of nowhere.

"What do you mean, 'Who's going to keep me safe'? *You* will, Ranger."

But what if she couldn't?

Stone poured a cup of strong coffee and looked out the kitchen window at the pasture and the fencing that needed mending. There was so much to do around here. The ranch needed painting, and the half bath's plumbing needed an overhaul. His quick fixes weren't cutting it.

His mom refused to sell, and truthfully, Stone didn't want to sell. He wanted to see the place thriving again with cattle to raise for beef, but money was tight and creditors called daily. Rhode had moved into the apartment above the garage six months ago. Bridge lived in a run-down cabin on the backside of the property. Way back when, they'd had cattlemen and ranch hands. Now it was just their hands and not enough to go around.

Sissy was trying to do private counseling as well as work for the team when they needed her and the scenes weren't bloody. Even though she lived two miles away in a small cottage, she spent most of her time here with Mama. Something was bothering his mom, but she was a private person. Stone guessed he inherited that trait from her.

Last night, he'd brought Emily here. To his home. He hadn't brought a woman home since he was in college. He'd given her the guest room upstairs. He wished he'd have put a security system in, but nothing terrible happened in Cedar Springs and rarely out this far.

But now bad things were happening, and if Emily was right about Paul Henderson, there was no telling who would come for them. A professional assassin. Hired thugs. Surely Paul wasn't killing women. Hadn't killed Paisley. Why? What motive would he have?

He glanced at the clock on the coffeepot. He had two hours before he needed to get ready for church. Mama was usually up before sunrise, especially on Sundays, but she'd been sleeping later. Sissy suspected she was depressed. Stone had no clue, but it ate away at him. He'd been keeping how far in debt they were to himself. He'd visited a few banks for loans, but it was a shaky time, and he couldn't seem to get one.

Last week he'd gone to the doc for his routine checkup, and his blood pressure was high. Dangerously. He had new meds for that and a strict warning to keep his cool.

Now he had this new information weighing on his shoulders, doing nothing for his blood pressure. He rubbed the tight knot in his shoulder and sipped his coffee. Until he knew for sure, he couldn't tell his family about Paisley. But Emily was here. How was he going to explain her?

"Hey." Rhode's deep, sleepy timbre drew him from his anxious thoughts. "I just saw that cute redhead from yesterday sitting on the back porch and her car out front. And since I know you're not that kind of guy…" He helped himself to a cup of coffee as he waited for an explanation.

Emily must have slipped out the back earlier

or had been out there long before Stone woke. He poured a cup of coffee and added sugar and a splash of cream. How sad was it he remembered how she drank her coffee from four years ago?

"She was attacked last night in conjunction with the case she was working at Judge's yesterday. She couldn't stay at her place so she followed me back here." Insisted she drive her own car.

"And why were you at her place?" His black eyebrows raised over his mug, his dark hair falling into his eyes.

"I wanted to know the details. Tiffany's death bugged us all."

Rhode opened the bread box and took out a loaf. "But you didn't see me or Bridge driving to wherever she lives." He popped two slices in the toaster. "She doesn't think Judge killed Tiff, does she? What would the motive be? I heard from Beau they had a prenup."

Leave it to Beau Brighton to spread gossip of the rich and famous. Beau was nothing but a spoiled rich kid who'd never grown up and never took anything seriously except well-bred horses and big-engine cars. Their sister Sissy could attest to that when Beau broke her heart years ago in high school. Stone had put his fist right through the punk's face. His daddy had the money to fix his nose. Stone had forgiven Beau, but he didn't pal around with him like Rhode. He'd been mad for a school year, but the following summer, they'd been back thick as thieves and had been ever since. Talk about betrayal to his sister—and twin sister at that!

"You're thinking about that time you busted up Beau's nose, aren't you?"

The toaster popped, and Rhode snagged his breakfast and the strawberry jam. "Beau's a cool dude once you get past the silver spoon. Anyway, the point is Judge had no motive. But as a judge, he has a lot of enemies. I'd sniff down that trail."

He sounded like the homicide detective he'd once been. Stone grunted his response to Rhode, then went out the kitchen door and around the wraparound porch to the back, where Emily sat in the wicker rocking chair, feet curled up under her and a Bible in hand. The air was crisp but not cold.

"I don't mean to interrupt your quiet time," he murmured and gently placed the coffee on the matching table beside her. He eased back toward the house to leave her to her time with the Lord. He respected and admired that she had it.

"You're not interrupting. I read my daily passage already. I was just enjoying the smell of the ranch—"

"We call that manure."

She chuckled, and he noticed her chin was

bruised, but the swelling had gone down on her cheek. "The smell of hay and grass and animals. Sunshine and peace." She grabbed her coffee and sipped but didn't remark on the fact that he'd remembered how she drank it when they had briefly worked together.

He eased down in the other rocker beside her and stretched out his legs. "We didn't talk much after we got back here last night. You mentioned three victims prior to Tiffany Williford but only went into detail about Deidre Dillion. Can you expound on Lexi Bryant and...and Paisley?"

After another sip, she turned her head, leaving it resting against the soft chair cushion. "Lexi Bryant died two years ago. Deidre last year. Did you know Lexi?"

Vaguely. "She was friends with Paisley and—"

"Coco Brighton."

Beau's sister. They lived on a huge dude ranch about forty minutes from Cedar Springs, but they kept condos in Austin, Dallas and Houston. Those were just the homes in Texas. Beau and Coco's family had vacation homes all over the world. Oil and cattle had made them multimillionaires.

"How is Lexi connected to the governor?" he asked. "Other than her dad being a fraternity brother of his."

"She worked as an admin assistant for the chair of the Texas Ethics Commission."

"Royce Pemberton."

She nodded. "She died in a car accident after a birthday bash for the governor, and she hung around the offices when Paisley worked his campaign. Side note: Royce Pemberton was also a fraternity brother, but I imagine you know this since your father was too. Her connection might not be her father as much as Royce."

The fraternity seemed to be a solid link. Or it could be that these women all ran in the same circles, and tragic things had ended their lives. Deidre might have had an affair, but there was no proof that he knew of implicating any of the other victims of sordid affairs. Only of personally knowing the governor in some capacity.

The governor might not be the killer—or the one ordering the kills. But to mention this to Emily now would only raise her hackles, and she already didn't trust him totally.

"Knowing what you do now, can you remain unbiased?" she asked.

"My sister might have been murdered, and someone is getting away with it. I can be unbiased. I want whoever is behind this, Emily. Governor or not. Have you or are you going to question him?"

"Not yet. I have to tread lightly, though someone knows I'm up to something. It's not a big secret anymore, but if I can keep it out of the media for now, that would be great. But when I feel I have more concrete evidence, yeah, I plan to talk to him. I don't expect the truth of course."

No, Paul would lie and have people continue to cover it up. But if he was not responsible and in the dark, he might have valuable information. Again, she wouldn't want to hear that at the moment. Instead he asked, "So what's the next step?"

"I'm still digging into the past, searching for women in their twenties to early thirties who died tragically or by suicide that connect to Paul Henderson and who had been around him or at an event where he was prior to their deaths, as well as links to his fraternity brothers. We might find more women. I don't know." She sipped her coffee again. "This is good, thank you."

Better a thank-you than calling him a bull-headed pig, which made zero sense. One was either bullheaded or pigheaded. He chuckled.

"What's so funny?"

"Nothing. I go to church on Sundays unless a cleanup requires my immediate attention. I see you're a believer too. Would you like to go to church with me?"

She tucked a lock of red hair shimmering with gold highlights behind her ear. "I would like that. I'd planned to attend somewhere so I packed for it."

"We leave at ten fifteen. It's not but a mile away or so." He stood. "After lunch we can figure out how we're going to make this dog hunt. Rhode's a PI and he could help—"

"No." She set her cup down with a clink. "No one but you, Stone."

His ire rose. "I know you probably heard the rumors about Rhode. He went through a bad spell, but he can be trusted. I trust him with my life."

"Well, I don't. And it has nothing to do with the rumors. Actually, that's not true. What I heard about your brother and the Cedar Springs PD is true. And he's good friends with Beau Brighton and Paul Henderson Junior, Stone. He might leak information."

"That's unfair, Emily." Stone's blood raced hot.

As if on cue, Rhode slipped around the corner in rumpled jeans and a faded blue T-shirt holding a cup of joe in his hand. "Mama's up. She wants to know if you want a roast or fried chicken for Sunday lunch." His tone was cool and he avoided eye contact with Emily. "I voted roast. But I guess my vote doesn't matter too much. Ranger O'Connell, what would you like for lunch?"

Oh, yeah. He'd overheard. His dander was up, but he'd brought a lot of the pain and mistrust on himself. Earning it all back and repairing his reputation would take time, and he was doing a good job of it. He'd been a great detective and he was a good man.

But even good guys sometimes stumbled and fell.

He was paying for those consequences.

"This was a bad idea," Emily said as she stood. "I'm going to pack up my things, and then I'm gone." She slipped by Stone and around Rhode when he didn't budge, then she entered the house.

Stone let out a breath. "Great."

"I did nothing wrong," Rhode said.

Stone arched an eyebrow. It was everything wrong he'd done that had earned Emily's distrust.

"Let me rephrase. I did nothing wrong today. It's not even 8:00 a.m." His sly smirk cooled Stone's jets and he sighed.

"I'll talk to her. She doesn't even fully trust me." Stone planned to remedy that.

"But she slept in your home and drank your coffee." Rhode whistled, and his two labs came running from the side of the house. "I have bacon, you rotten rascals."

Stone left Rhode feeding his dogs and licking his wounds and entered the house. Emily hadn't made it upstairs. Mama had intercepted her.

After introducing her properly and settling on a roast for lunch, he followed her upstairs.

"Emily, please stay. If you don't want Rhode involved, fine. But you're not safe on your own."

"Let's just get past church."

"Fair enough."

He left her, and by ten, she came downstairs and took his breath away. She wore a long green dress with salmon-colored flowers, and her hair was in a soft knot atop her head, a few strands framing her face. His throat turned dry, and he scratched the back of his neck.

"You look really pretty," he said, feeling like a complete heel.

"Thank you. So do you." She smirked and passed by him, her sweet vanilla scent dizzying him. He glanced down at his khaki pants and pale blue dress shirt.

"Men aren't pretty," he called as she closed the back door.

Rhode came downstairs looking like a decent human being in black pants and a white dress shirt, sleeves rolled to the elbows. "I'll drive Mama. Figure your guest probably don't want to be in the same vehicle with me."

Emily entered again, her cheeks tinted pink. "Rhode, I didn't mean to offend you."

"No?"

"No. Mostly because I didn't expect you to

hear me." She slightly shrugged and Rhode actually chuckled.

The woman had a way of charming people when insulting them. He was a *bullheaded pig* after all.

"I guess that's fair." Rhode glanced at Stone, then shoved his hands in his pockets. "Maybe you don't think you can trust me, and that's fine. But you can. Now my brother is involved, and I would never risk his life. He's done too much and taken a proverbial bullet for me on more than one occasion. So if for no other reason, believe me, Ranger O'Connell."

She politely nodded. "I do believe that, Rhode. And you can call me Emily."

"I think I'll stick with Ranger O'Connell. I only call friends by their first name, and you've made it pretty clear we're not friends." He slipped by her and out the front door.

Emily winced. "Well, that was uncomfortable."

Stone swallowed down the emotion from hearing Rhode's words.

"Also, are y'all purposely named after ways to get from one place to another? Stone. Rhode. Bridge."

He cocked his head, confused. "You just offended my brother, and now you're insulting our names?"

"I also plan to eat a roast with you for lunch." She cradled her Bible, which had a salmon-colored sweater that matched the flowers on her dress draped over it.

"I don't know if I want to hug you or hit you." He grabbed his keys and grinned.

"How about neither." Her brown eyes sparkled and he shook his head. "Your mom asked me to please stay for lunch, and I didn't have the heart to say no. So I'll stay, then I'll be on my way."

"I wish you'd reconsider," he said as he locked the door behind him.

"You really trust your brother?" she asked as they got into the truck and buckled up.

"I do."

"I'll think about it. That's the best I can offer you right now."

Better than a no. "I will not let you down, Emily. Neither will my brothers."

He prayed he could live up to those words.

He inserted the key into the ignition and heard the click.

His gut clenched and his heart lurched into his throat. "Get out of the truck! Now!"

THREE

Emily's heart leaped into her throat as she shoved open the truck door just as the hood from the vehicle exploded sky-high and a rush of heat thrust her from the cab and into the air. She landed on the ground with a thud. Ears ringing, dazed and disoriented, she curled into a fetal position, hoping to protect herself from the metal truck bits and debris raining down on her.

A bomb. Someone had planted a bomb, and not in her car but Stone's truck.

Stone! Had he made it out of the truck? Was he safe?

A second blast shot flames above the trees, and the front of the truck went up in smoke. Scrambling for the large tree to take cover, she scoured the area for any sign of Stone, but he was nowhere.

How did anyone know she was here? Had her attacker from last night lay in wait to follow her?

Thoughts zinged through her mind like bullets from a machine gun. She coughed and sputtered, the smoke black and thick like smog.

The house hadn't been touched, and she thanked God for that. Emily had brought danger to the Spencer home. What if his mom had been in that truck? His brother? She'd never have forgiven herself.

Where was Stone?

"Emily!" he called, and her racing heart took relief in his voice.

"Over here," she hollered and waved, signaling to her position behind the tree.

Sprinting from the back end of the truck, his face dirty and his clean church clothes ruined, Stone slid like a baseball player into home base and sidled up next to her, placing his hands on her face, her head. "Are you okay? You hurt?"

Her back was gonna feel it tomorrow, her head ached and his voice sounded underwater, but she was in one piece. "I think so, for being bombed that is. It was a bomb, right?"

Stone gripped her hand. "Yeah. It was definitely a bomb. I didn't think we'd have time once I heard the click. We skated by through the skin of our teeth."

Leaning her head against the rough bark, she coughed again. "I'm glad you noticed the sound. If the radio had been on, we wouldn't have heard it."

"Good thing I ride in silence." He squeezed her hand, then released it. "I think it's pretty obvious that the deaths you're looking into are homicides, and whoever is behind them knows you know. Now they're aware I also know. They picked my truck, not your car."

Emily regretted involving him for safety's sake. "I'm sorry, Stone."

"Don't be." He swiped his sweaty brow with the back of his hand. "I all but forced you into it."

"Except I can't be forced to do anything."

His eyebrows raised. "We've been bombed and you want to argue."

He had a point. "Arguing takes my mind off being scared." Time to get real. "And I'm scared, Stone. Not enough to back down or go underground, but I'm not so stupid to be unaware of the serious danger I'm in or the fact that these attempts won't stop. One of these days, I'll start a car and I won't escape." Her voice trembled, and she hated that it made her appear weak. She wasn't. But the governor had seriously deep pockets and a limitless reach. She was only one female Texas Ranger.

"Can I be honest then too? I'm concerned. But more than ever, it solidifies that you're not barking up the wrong tree. These women—my sister—were murdered. These were no accidents or self-inflicted deaths. We have to get to the truth."

But it might kill them. They were in big-time trouble.

"I can't stay."

"You have to stay."

Stone frowned and held up his finger. "We'll discuss this further, but now I need the fire department." He called it in and ended the call as a red Ford truck pulled into the driveway, and Bridge jumped out and came running. He was in dark dress jeans and a red polo shirt. Not as dressed up as the other two brothers, maybe he was going to church, maybe not.

The truck blazed and Stone frowned. "Let's back away. It could blow if the fire reaches the gas tank." At the moment, flames were raging over the hood and the cab of the truck.

As they took cover closer to the driveway, Bridge asked, "What happened?" He glanced at the burning truck. "Who bombed you?" His eyes narrowed and he gazed at Emily. "What are you doing here? Is this about your case? Where's Mama and Rhode? Is Sissy here? Somebody give me some answers!"

Impatience pretty much summed up Bridge Spencer. His amber eyes lasered in on his older brother and his nostrils flared. He was worried. Afraid. And it filtered out in frustration and anger. Emily understood.

Stone laid a hand on his brother's broad shoulder. "Mama is with Rhode at church, and Sissy, I assume, is there too. We don't know who bombed the truck." He looked to Emily for permission to divulge more information, and she feared if she said she wasn't at liberty to say, Bridge might throttle her and Stone might too. Rightly so. His family had been endangered.

But she couldn't be as forthcoming as they wanted regardless of the fact that the governor was on to them. The less his family knew, the safer they were. "I think it's in relation to my case, which unfortunately is classified."

His mouth dropped and he looked at Stone as if she'd said she bombed the truck herself. "Do you know what's going on?"

Stone nodded.

"But I can't know?"

"No."

Bridge threw his hands in the air as sirens whirred, signaling their approach.

"Scale of one to ten. Ten being the worst," Bridge said and raked a hand through his hair, but since he already wore the intentionally messy look, it didn't make it any messier.

"Eight," Stone said with a don't-hit-me look.

"Eight! Eight and I can't know?" He slapped his hand against his chest and stormed toward the flaming mess. Firefighters went to work dousing flames. Emily followed Stone and Bridge to the debris and watched as Bridge examined the site. "Professional. Intended to kill the targets, not anyone else. Two blasts?"

"Yes. How do you know?" Emily asked.

"It's *classified*," he returned with a heavy dose of sarcasm. He whipped out his phone and marched toward the back of the house for privacy.

"So, he's mad," she said. She couldn't blame the guy. His brother could have been killed or any family member that might have been inside the vehicle. *Classified* wasn't a word a Spencer man would want to hear at any time, but especially not today.

"My brothers have skills that can help us."

"You sound like Liam Neeson's character in all those movies."

"You watched all those movies?" he asked as he picked debris out of her hair.

She swatted his hand away. She could pick junk out of her hair alone. She at least had that much control. "It's classified."

He snorted. "He's not used to being out of the loop."

Didn't appear any of the Spencer brothers liked being out of the loop. All were take-charge guys apparently. "What's his FBI background? How would he know it was two blasts?"

"He worked as an FBI special agent with CIRG."

The Critical Incidence Response Group. They handled negotiations, bombs, profiles. The list was long, but Stone didn't offer which specialized unit Bridge had worked with or why he was no longer part of the bureau. "Who's he calling?"

"I don't know, and I highly suggest you don't ask him." Stone rubbed his temples as the paramedics approached.

Cedar Springs Police pulled in behind the ambulance and fire truck. Firefighters had already snuffed out the blaze since the bomb had been strategically set to stay contained. Emily allowed the paramedics to treat her but declined going to the hospital, and Stone declined any treatment and was now talking with an officer as another patrolman secured the home with yellow crime scene tape.

His family wasn't going to appreciate coming home to this disaster.

She called George to fill him in and see what he wanted to do from here, but his phone went to voicemail after five rings. Emily approached Stone, who was watching his brother pace near the side of the house, his phone to his ear.

"I called George. No answer, but it's Sunday, and he golfs on Sundays."

Stone pivoted. "Emily, I need to tell my brothers. They can help. Bridge has FBI connections and Rhode is a PI and a good detective. He also has some insider connections—"

"Which could be on the take. We can't afford inside people knowing anything."

"Okay. What if he doesn't actually ask questions? He's still great friends with PJ and Beau Brighton and even the Ethics Commission chair's son, Trystan. They know stuff, and they love to talk about stuff their parents do. Please let me share the situation with just the family."

She didn't want to. Especially not with Rhode, since his friendships with the elite were tight. But what choice did she have? She wanted to trust Stone. Her heart told her she could, but there was that stupid insecurity now. *Thanks, Dad.* "Okay, Stone. But do you think it's smart to stay on the ranch? They know we're here."

"If it's a professional hit, they'll find us anywhere. I have a better advantage here, and now that I'm aware, and we can get Rhode and Bridge involved, then we can do better at guarding the property and the home."

Emily bit the inside of her lower lip. "What about your mom? Maybe we need to get her somewhere else safe."

"I agree, but we get our stubbornness from her. So I don't see her agreeing to go stay with Sissy or anywhere else. But I'll press it."

Emily ran her palms down the sides of her hips. "If everyone is on board, I'll stay."

"And not change your mind or threaten to leave? I can't have that kind of anxiety. I need to know you're going to stick it out." His gaze bore into hers, but she held it.

"I'm going to stick it out. You have my word. But I'm the lead investigator, and you have to remember you're helping, not taking over a case. I need to know you're going to let me call the shots and not go renegade or Team Spencer with your bros."

He stuck out a filthy hand. "Deal. You wanna spit and make it official?"

She scrunched her nose. "I'll pass."

"Then you have my word. My word is good. It's all I got really."

Her stomach dropped. Dad had said similar words. Vain, empty words. *God, please let Stone Spencer live up to his word and not make me look and feel like a fool again.* She hesitantly placed her hand in his and felt the firm confidence and promise in it.

"Deal."

But could she trust *all* the Spencer brothers?

Stone's truck had been taken to the impound for Cedar Springs CSI to thoroughly comb it, and a bomb squad out of Austin was coming to take a look thanks to Bridge's phone call to a friend. By the time church ended and Mama and Sissy arrived, nothing was left but the smell of burnt rubber and oil.

Sissy had immediately hugged Emily and escorted her inside to have a cup of tea and talk about her feelings. Stone had chuckled because Emily didn't seem like a feelings-talking kind of woman unless she was peeved. But she had admitted to him she was scared, and that, to him, was a sign of strength. If someone wasn't afraid, he'd be worried about their mental health. The person behind these attacks had power and influence and ways to hide their dealings. It was scary.

Mama had insisted on staying on the ranch, and she'd made that crystal clear when she went to work on lunch as if there hadn't been a bomb. After lunch, Stone brought a pot of coffee and a tray of cups and condiments into the family room and placed them on the coffee table. Rhode and Bridge sat on the couch facing the piano, and Stone sat in one of the comfy chairs next to them. Sissy and Emily had yet to appear, and Mama was going to stay out of this portion. She knew what she needed to know. Stone would carry the rest of the weight.

Bridge leaned forward, resting his elbows on his knees. "My guy from the bomb squad just arrived at the impound. He's gonna check it out now. See if he can find any telling signatures. The fact that it was two blasts reminds me of this—" He stopped short as Emily and Sissy entered the family room. Sissy was still dressed in a pink flowy dress, her two Blenheim Cavalier King Charles therapy spaniels trailing her heels. Stone liked Louis and Lady, but he preferred Rhode's labs. They liked to romp hard and wrestle.

Emily had cleaned up and put on a pair of worn jeans that fit her better than they should and a blue V-neck T-shirt. Her hair was hanging past her shoulders and still damp. No makeup. Man, she was crazy beautiful. To keep from gawking, he poured a cup of coffee. Emily sat on the piano bench, and Sissy took the chair opposite him. Louis laid by her feet, but Lady curled up at Emily's side. She grinned and scooped her up, scratched her ears then placed a kiss to her Blenheim spot on her head. He'd never wished to be a dog so much.

"What were you saying, Bridge?" Emily asked.

"Oh, just that two blasts about two minutes apart was a signature of a bomber named Kerry Von Meter. He was a bomb-for-hire guy and could be reached through the dark web. We're talking big money. FBI finally got him about two years ago, and he was supposed to give them the names of his employers for a lessened sentence, but he disappeared from a sting operation, where he'd been wired. The guy in the bomb unit in Austin used to work CIRG but came home— anyway—he's going to check it out himself and see if it could be Kerry Von Meter's work."

Stone sipped the black brew. "Will that give us any idea who he's working for or just that someone with big money hired him? Because we already know that."

"But *we* don't," Bridge said and looked to Emily.

She gently put Lady on the floor and stood, sliding her hands into her back pockets. Even that was distracting. Stone cleared his throat and looked elsewhere, catching his sister's eye. Sissy gave him a mischievous grin, and her twin got the sixth sense and eyed him too. Now it was getting embarrassing.

"The reason I'm not at liberty to say anything—but am going to now even without my director's okay—is because we believe Governor Henderson is a murderer."

"Paul?" Rhode said and scoffed.

"That right there is another reason I didn't want you to know," Emily said.

Rhode frowned. "Forgive me for being shocked."

"Who do you think he murdered? And why?" Bridge asked, ignoring the tension heating up the room.

Now it was going to get complicated. Emily peered at him. "Stone, why don't you tell them?" Compassion swirled in her soft brown eyes, and he never appreciated her more. News of Paisley's possible murder would be easier to take coming from him.

"What I'm about to say cannot be told to Mama. Not yet. Not until we are one hundred percent sure."

Everyone nodded and agreed. Stone relayed the information Emily had given him last night, everything from Tiffany's death to looking into old cases. Deidre Dillion, Lexi Bryant and... Paisley.

The room silenced and the air thickened. Sissy cried, and both pups jumped in her lap to offer comfort.

Finally, Rhode broke the silence. "Why would Paul—Governor Henderson—kill Paisley or any of these women? We need motive."

"Did they have dirt on him about his affairs? Did they all have affairs with him? Not Paisley. No way." Bridge stood and massaged the nape of his neck.

Emily cleared her throat. "It doesn't appear that anyone except Deidre Dillion had a romantic relationship with the governor. But working for him or knowing him closely would have given them access to information he might not have wanted them to have. We're working to make more connections, but we must tread lightly."

"Yeah, because if it's not him, and we throw out accusations of murder, it won't matter if we've been family friends, he'll make sure we're slapped with a slander lawsuit we'll never get out from under. Ever. And that's just for starters." Rhode jumped up and began pacing by the window. "I never thought Pai killed herself. But I never dug."

Stone crossed the room and laid a hand on his shoulder. "None of us did. And none of us wanted to believe it. We will find the truth. We won't stop until we get justice for her and for all these women."

"Where do we start?" Bridge asked.

Emily's shoulders relaxed. "We have a loose connection that could be a coincidence. All these women are linked by someone who was a fraternity brother with Paul Henderson. There might not be any other motive. It might just be good hunting ground."

"Your words make me think *serial killer*, not someone picking off people who might know dirty laundry he doesn't want aired out," Bridge said. "You're profiling him."

Stone had wondered himself why women who

were connected or related to fraternity brothers were targets. "It could be a vendetta, not a serial killer hunting prey. I'm not ready to make that leap."

Emily agreed and turned to Bridge. "Since you clearly have a background in profiling, maybe you need to profile this case. The victims are all around the same age, have the frat connection and have been near Henderson often, especially within days and even hours of their deaths. So we very well could be dealing with a serial killer. Or a vendetta of some sort. I agree."

"I need more information besides a frat connection, but it's a start." Bridge made notes in his phone.

Rhode blew a heavy breath. "If Paul Henderson is a serial killer, then we'll find murders before now. If we don't, then it's likely another motive."

"So, PI that angle," Emily said coolly.

"I will," Rhode said with equal chill.

"So far, the same ME has signed off on the reports for Deidre, Lexi and Paisley," Emily said. "My guess is he's in the governor's pocket. Others in the office may be too, or they could have been threatened in order to turn a blind eye."

"Do we want to apply pressure to them this soon? Getting someone to flip isn't going to be easy," Stone said.

"If anyone will know what the governor is up to, it's going to be his chief of staff. Martin Landers," Sissy said. "We've been friends since college. I could meet up with him for lunch." She wiped her eyes again.

Emily cocked her head. "If he knows what the governor is doing, he'll know someone is trying to kill your brother and that you now know this too. It's risky."

Sissy's face reddened. "I don't think he knows the governor is murdering women or having them killed, but it won't be suspicious, because he calls me at least once a month to catch up. I usually refrain because he's married, but I know he has lunch alone at the Guittiere Club on Tuesdays to destress. Been doing that for ages. I could happen to be there. He'd ask me to sit down. And since I'm already there, I could…for a minute or two."

Rhode frowned. "I don't like that. He's always been slimy."

"It's lunch, Rhode. One of us can be nearby or outside with earwigs," Bridge added.

Wow, this is getting covert. Boys with their toys. "Go through with it, but only if you feel comfortable and it won't tip him off."

Sissy nodded. "It'll be fine. We're friends and I don't think he's a bad guy. If he had knowledge of Governor Henderson's crimes, he would be quick to call the police."

Stone wasn't so sure. Money talked. Everyone had their tipping point. Almost everyone anyway. "Rhode, if you're looking into the governor's past and possible other crimes, who is going to work more recent deaths that might be homicides?"

"I will," Bridge said. He directed his explanation to Emily. "I have friends that can be trusted, and I won't tell them why I need access to the cases. Should I stick to Austin since that appears to be where the women are dying? Except for Tiffany Williford. She died in Cedar Springs. Our coroner did that report."

"And failed to get it right. Consider him compromised, but yes, stick to the Austin area or surrounding places the governor goes, like his lake house or his cabin." Emily turned to Stone. "I want us to meet with the governor's wife. You think she's a little salty over her husband's infidelities?"

"Maybe, but prestige and money mean more." Stone shrugged. "We may get nowhere, but we need to try. Informally." He turned to Bridge and Rhode. "Getting a list of the fraternity brothers will be important. See if any women connected to them but not the governor went missing or died, and it was ruled an accident or suicide."

"Good. I agree." Emily's face brightened at his

suggestion, and for weird reasons, it swelled in his chest. "He attended Vanderbilt Law."

"But he went to the University of Texas at Austin first," Stone said. "That's where the fraternity brothers are from. My dad didn't attend law school, and I don't think Mayor Dillion did either. But I know they were in the Delta Tau Delta fraternity."

Her phone rang. She held up a finger. "It's my boss's boss." She answered the call from the deputy director. "Ranger O'Connell, sir." She listened, and then her cheeks blanched, and she collapsed on the piano bench. "When? Are you sure?" She listened again. "Okay. Yes. Thank you, sir." She ended the call.

"What's going on?" Stone asked.

"My director, George Baldwin, was in a car accident coming home from the golf course in Austin about thirty minutes ago. He was killed."

Stone's blood froze. "But it wasn't a car accident, was it?"

Emily stared vacantly at the phone, then peered up at him. "I don't think so."

FOUR

Emily's mind reeled as she slowly entered the Spencer Ranch home. The smells from the earlier lunch of roast and potatoes permeated the atmosphere. The sun was tucked in for the night, and the house was lit with candles. She noticed there was no Christmas tree. She'd put hers up the first week in November. Christmas was her favorite time, especially when her dad was home, which was every other year. He was a long-haul truck driver and was gone weeks at a time. Looking back, he was splitting his time between families. One year with them, one year with the other family.

Her cell phone felt heavy in her pocket, knowing there were voicemails from her half sister, Dottie. Did she want to talk to Dottie? No. She could not hear about her perfect life and how much she'd been doted on by her father. Emily's father. It was too much. Instead, she'd let the texts go unread and the deleted voicemails unheard.

After finding out about George's death, they'd driven to the scene and asked around at the golf course about George's day and if he'd spoken to anyone or if it appeared anyone had been following him. No one knew anything. Then she'd gone to the office and talked with the deputy director. He was putting one of her colleagues in as interim chief. She'd asked for some vacation time—no point bringing anyone in. The less they knew, the safer they'd be.

"You hungry?" Stone asked.

Emily's stomach rumbled. "I am."

Shuffling sounded and Mrs. Spencer entered the room in her fluffy pink robe and matching slippers. "I thought I heard you come in. Who's hungry? I'll fix us some leftovers. Sound good?"

"Mama, you don't have to serve us. We can take care of it. Go on to bed. You look tired anyway."

"Well, I want to." She ignored her eldest and winked at Emily. "I'm still a mama. Bridge was looking for you earlier. He's bunking in his old room tonight after what happened today. Couldn't make him leave. Sissy's here too."

Emily followed her into the kitchen. "Can I help, Mrs. Spencer? It's the least I can do. I brought so much trouble—"

"Nonsense," Mrs. Spencer said. "I may not have had real bombs going off on this ranch before, but the boys were walking bombs every day. And call me Marisol. Please." She laughed and tucked her dark hair behind her ear. She wore it chin length, and while she was likely in her late sixties, there wasn't an ounce of gray. Her bronzed skin had been passed down to her children, though only the twins, Rhode and Sissy, had her jet-black hair and eyes, sharp cheek bones and symmetrical lines. Emily imagined in her younger years she'd looked a lot like an exotic actress.

"I imagine the house was loud. I always wanted siblings, but now I don't," she said with a sour note. As if her dad's other daughter felt her thoughts, her phone vibrated. Emily wasn't answering. She hit the side button twice to send it to voicemail.

"Sibling squabble going on?" Marisol asked.

"No. Nothing to squabble about." She shrugged and pocketed her phone. "I'm an only child."

Marisol arched an eyebrow and pulled the leftover roast from the fridge, and Emily found the cabinets with plates and retrieved three of them in case Stone's mom was hungry too.

"Or I thought I was." She told Marisol what she'd recently discovered. "I haven't told anyone that." It felt good telling Marisol. She reminded her of her own mom in many ways but was unbiased.

"You know, you should take the call. She didn't know about you either and might need support too. Maybe you need one another." She plated the food and popped the dish in the microwave. "I can't imagine all the feelings you're having. I'm so sorry. But I think the ill feelings need to go where they should, and Dottie isn't that source." She handed her a warm plate of roast and all the fixins then plated another and repeated the heating process.

Stone entered the kitchen along with Bridge. Those two looked more like their father and Stone must have gotten his green eyes from him. Not sure where his perpetual scowl originated.

"Smells good," he said and sat at the table as Marisol placed a plate in front of him.

"Tea or water?" she asked.

"Mama, I can get my own drink. I'm almost forty."

She ignored him and brought a pitcher of tea to the table and set it beside him. "Bridge, you hungry, baby?"

"I can get my own dinner too."

"Is that a yes?"

He sighed and collapsed in a chair by Stone. "Sure, Mama." He grinned at Stone and he returned it. Apparently they were used to their mother's stubbornness.

"It's delicious," Emily said. "I can't tell you the last time I had a home-cooked meal before today."

"You don't cook?" Marisol asked.

"She burns it," Stone said, "in love." He snickered, and she tossed him an annoyed look, but inside she smiled. He was referring to her dish towel.

Emily ran her roll through a rich brown gravy. "I'll have you know I don't burn everything. I never cared much about cooking growing up. I wanted to be outside riding bikes or playing kickball at the park with the boys. I was a total tomboy."

Marisol handed Bridge a plate of food, and he kissed her hand, then squeezed it. "Sissy was running around like one of the boys too. Until she turned sixteen and things changed."

Bridge snorted. "Yeah, instead of running with them she wanted to kiss 'em."

Stone's eyebrows raised, and a smirk cued Emily that he was in full agreement, and the brothers had fun childhood secrets about their sister.

"Oh, stop. She had one major crush." Marisol put a kettle of water on the stove.

"Yeah. Glad that never went anywhere," Stone

said and ran his roast through his gravy. "Beau Brighton was nothing but a heartbreaker and a spoiled rich kid who was never told no."

Bridge nodded. "Sometimes I wonder how Rhode could still be friends with him—although there was that summer and fall he cut him off cold turkey." He shrugged and buttered a roll. "But then the next summer, they were like brothers and—" Bridge glanced at Emily, now seemingly aware she was in the room. "Anyway it's water under the—" He stopped.

She grinned. "No, go ahead. Say it."

He returned her smile and popped the roll in his mouth, then pointed. "Can't talk with a full mouth," he mumbled through the yeasty bread but managed a wink. Emily guessed he wasn't holding a grudge for her cutting him out earlier in the investigation. Rhode was a different story altogether, and while she didn't fully trust any of them, she trusted Rhode least of all, but she couldn't quite put her finger on why.

The men and Marisol reminisced about childhood days, and Emily enjoyed the stories, banter and teasing. Her family dinners had been pretty quiet and often on trays in front of the TV when it was just her and Mom. Even when Dad was home and they gathered at the table, it was polite conversation. No teasing or rowdiness. Not bad. Just different. Her phone rang again and she glanced at it.

Dottie Jackson. That was the surname her father had used under the alias of Ward Jackson. At least Emily had gotten the real identity of her father. Marisol gave her a knowing look and Emily's cheeks heated. Stone raised an eyebrow.

She let it go to voicemail and shrugged. Marisol patted her shoulder. "Dirty in the dishwasher," she said then kissed each son on the top of their heads. "I'm turning in."

They said their goodnights, and Marisol's footsteps creaking the hardwood floor joists could be heard as she padded off to her bedroom.

"I like your mom." Emily rinsed her plate and put it and her fork in the dishwasher.

"We do too," Bridge said. "Now that she's out of earshot, how did it go looking into your boss's death?"

Emily's stomach flopped over. "Nothing but dead ends. I can't say anything either. It's up to me to get justice."

Stone's mouth hardened. "I get that, Emily, but we might need to bring in some other sources, federally, to help with this—or even other Texas Rangers."

"No. The governor has a far and wide reach. We don't know if other Rangers are compromised or anyone at the federal level. Reaching out can put other people's lives in danger too. Serious danger. I can't in good conscience do that." Not to mention if trusted sources came in, money talked and Paul Henderson had a lot of it. He was from old money to begin with, and his reach in the business and political world went far beyond being the governor of Texas. He hobnobbed with some of the most renowned business leaders, politicians and even Hollywood stars. No. Absolutely not.

Stone exchanged a grim look with Bridge, then let out a long, slow sigh. "Okay. We do it your way, Emily."

She got the impression he left off "for now."

"Sissy will meet with Martin Landers, the chief of staff, for lunch," Stone said. "She chose to call him. Let him know she'll be in the area and wanted to see if he'd have time to get together for a lunch. It worked."

Emily nodded. "We'll be there too then."

After Stone and Bridge had a slice of lemon meringue pie and they chitchatted some more, she excused herself to bed. She trudged up the stairs, the exhaustion of the day catching up as the adrenaline ebbed. She wanted nothing more than to crawl under soft sheets and let the lull of sleep take over.

Once she'd dressed for bed, she slid into the covers. She played Dottie's newest voicemail.

"Hey, Emily. It's me, Dottie. I'm not trying to be pushy. I get if you don't want to talk to me or my brother. I just—I'd like to meet you and talk. Anyway, here's my number again, but you know that by now. Thanks." Then the line went dead.

What could she possibly want to talk about? How great her childhood had been? How much she'd loved their dad? Emily could admit she was jealous and being a bit childish. Marisol was right. Dottie wasn't to blame for what her dad did. But that didn't make Emily any less angry, jealous, confused or hurt. She couldn't promise she wouldn't say anything ugly in their meeting—and that wouldn't be fair to Dottie. Honestly, she wasn't ready for any of this. Mom had mentioned they were in this alone and together— that his other family could fend for themselves. Mom was all she had. She couldn't betray her.

Wouldn't.

A notification on her phone buzzed, and she glanced at the screen, her heart lurching into her throat. She had three notifications, but she must have missed them during all the talk at the table. This was just like before she was attacked in her apartment. It was from her security cam app, notifying her of movement inside her apartment.

She opened the app icon and clicked Live Camera, and her apartment bedroom came into view. Standing in front of the camera was a person clad all in black, including a ski mask and a pair of dark lenses underneath, blocking out his eyes. He was up close, staring right at her through the camera.

Adrenaline returned and raced through her veins, fear pulsing with every heartbeat. He ran his index finger across his neck in a slow slicing motion, then sprinted from her bedroom, which he'd tossed. She checked the cams in the kitchen, living room and small home office, which was really no bigger than a large pantry. Every single room had been ripped apart. He was probably looking for evidence against the governor.

She went back to the video of the intruder and replayed it.

Watched him run his index finger across his neck.

The threatening message was clear.

She was dead.

Stone sat with his head in his hands at the kitchen table. His skin felt hot. His blood pressure was up. He recognized the signs: headaches, fatigue and chest pain. So much for keeping calm and not enduring too much stress. Stone had a sick feeling that things were only going to go from bad to worse. Not telling Mama about Paisley was eating away at him. She deserved to know. The fact that they were being targeted while investigating these women was solid enough for him to believe Emily's theory was on target. But it wouldn't hold up in court. Not yet.

It didn't help that he couldn't reach out to law enforcement friends for additional help.

Emily was leading this investigation, and she trusted no one. He got that. Paul's reach was wide. Ocean kind of wide. Stone didn't know who could or couldn't be trusted either. But surely, there were good guys out there. The Rangers he'd worked with were standup guys, but Emily had a point. Money was mighty tempting and greed was present in everyone. If someone offered him the money to fix the ranch, buy more cattle and get it up and going, he couldn't deny he'd be tempted.

But he'd flee the temptation. God would provide for them. He always had, but it was hard to stay out of God's way and let Him do it.

Stone put his plate in the dishwasher and downed a couple of pain relievers for his headache when he felt Emily's presence. It was weird how he knew it was her and not anyone else. He turned and noticed her skin was washed out and her eyes wide.

"What's wrong?" he asked.

"I'll let you see for yourself." She held out her phone and pressed Play. He watched as a masked intruder made a death threat. His gut tightened and his blood whooshed.

Hello, stress.

"He's ransacked your place. Any files or information about the governor or the victims there?"

"No. George has it all. Had. George had it." The sorrow in her voice pinched his chest.

He reached out for her, hesitated, then let his fingers glide through a strand of her hair. Losing someone you cared about was painful. "I know you're tired. I am too, but we need to go to George's and check it ourselves. Camera Guy might have already hit it first, or he's on his way now. We could beat him to the punch. It's worth a shot."

"I know. That's why I'm not in my pajamas anymore."

The thought of seeing her in cute pajamas was interesting but one he wouldn't entertain. Completely inappropriate. "I'll get my keys. We can take the work truck. It's not as nice as my personal one was though. Still, it works."

Once they were in the truck, Emily put George's address into her phone, and they made it there in thirty-two minutes. His house was in a quiet suburb outside Austin. Lights were out and the street silent. Stone made a pass around the block just to surveil, then he parked a few houses down.

"He got family?" Stone asked.

"No. He's divorced and no kids."

"Let's look around, see if any entry point has been breached." The man was deceased, but they had no legal claim to be inside. This was more than a covert mission—it was an illegal one. If they were caught, they could wind up in jail.

Emily agreed, and they kept to the shadows as they made their way to George's house. After clearing the yard, they checked for entry points breached. Nothing looked tampered with, but the kitchen door was unlocked. It could be an accident or something more sinister. Stone pulled his gun and Emily followed suit.

"Back me up," he said.

"Roger that."

Stone entered the dark one-story home's kitchen, the smell of something garlicky still lingering. The kitchen was intact. They cleared it and moved into the open living room, which was also untouched. It looked like they beat Emily's intruder here. Unless he was counting on that and planned to ambush them. Stone stayed on high alert.

George was a neat and tidy man. Everything had a place; even the TV remotes were lined up on the coffee table. Half the time, Stone couldn't find his.

After clearing the rest of the home, they went into George's office, which was the most likely place he'd keep files or photos in regards to the case. On the wall behind his desk were two four-drawer filing cabinets the color of sand. "I'll take one, you take the other," he said.

Emily nodded, used her Maglite and went to work combing through them.

Thankfully, George's house wasn't on top of his neighbors, and there were mature trees between the lots. Flashlight beams shouldn't arouse anyone from sleep or call attention to night owls who were still awake. Stone methodically searched through each drawer file by file. He found cases George had worked that had gone cold, along with tax information, business stuff. Nothing that stood out. He went through all four drawers on his filing cabinet and frowned.

"Nothing here."

Emily was on her third drawer, the Maglite wedged between her teeth, giving her two free hands. "Unh-eh ere," she said.

He grinned but deciphered her cumbered words.

Nothing here.

He looked around George's office. If Stone wanted to hide top-secret information, would he even keep it in the office? Seemed like the best choice—close to him. But he had to know someone might look here, so he could have rented a deposit box or used a locker. But then George had obviously been smart and might have deduced that someone savvy would think of that too and look elsewhere. So maybe he did leave it here. Ugh. His thoughts were like the iocaine powder scene in *The Princess Bride*. Clearly he would not put the poison in his own cup. Or he would. *Grr...*

"I'm going to look elsewhere. Be right back," Stone said.

Emily removed the light from her lips. "If this were a horror movie, you sealed your fate with those words. No one ever comes back after saying they'll be back."

He liked that she could still have humor in such a dark moment. They needed it. Their jobs were grisly, and without some joking, it would be too much to bear. He allowed her the coping mechanism. "Well, this isn't a horror movie. It's action adventure. So just call me the Terminator."

"I never liked those movies," she said dryly.

He snorted. "Maybe not. But he did come back. Until the franchise was wrung dry."

She laughed as he left the room and stood in the hall.

"Where would he hide important information?" he asked.

Would he even keep it here in the house? If they couldn't retrieve anything, they'd have to start looking into lockers and safe deposit boxes and storage units. He wouldn't keep it at the office. That would be too easy to access, even in a locked cabinet. And a man like George would keep records. Stone would have.

He walked the floors, listening as joists creaked. Loose boards. He searched behind wall art and in cabinets. Even under the lid of the toilet tank. He ran his hands inside cabinets and closets. Nothing.

Emily found him in the bedroom as he lay on the floor feeling underneath the bed. "Nothing in the filing cabinets."

"Nothing under here but dust bunnies. I'm going to need an allergy pill when we get back to the ranch." Stone scooted out from under the bed and shone his light in the closet. "I looked in there already. Nothing but golf shirts, work clothes, shoes and his bowling bag."

Emily narrowed her eyes. "George doesn't bowl."

Stone frowned as he crawled into the closet and retrieved the bowling bag. He unzipped it and found a twenty-pound bowling ball. "You sure?"

"I'm sure."

Stone removed the bowling ball, placed it on the bed and began to feel around inside the bag. "Hold the phone," he said as his fingers touched a hidden zipper and undid it, then pulled out a file. "What do we have here?"

He opened the manila file and photos of the governor with Tiffany Williford, Deidre Dillion and Lexi Bryant spilled out. All in conversation. Nothing to prove an affair or fight, but the time stamps were all within days of their deaths.

"These must be the photos Ranger McElroy pulled from the iCloud once he started building a case to bring to PIU. All he needed to do was search the governor's name or the parties or enter the dates, and photos that had been marked Public would surface." Then came the work of sifting through them.

Emily sighed. "And they got the poor guy killed."

"Yeah. Seems like they did." He flipped through a few more, then froze.

Governor Paul Henderson was laughing with his sister Paisley at a party of some kind. Seemed pretty casual in dress code. But his hand was on her arm, and she seemed comfortable with him.

His throat turned dry and he couldn't swallow.

Emily leaned over him and pointed to the time stamp. The day before she died. "He's either got reason to silence these women, or he's strategically stalking them. Does the fact that they have ties to a frat brother have anything to do with it?"

"I don't know," he mumbled and stared at the

photo of his sister. She had been beautiful. Full of life and laughter. Big dreams. Big heart. It didn't matter if there was a connection. If Paul Henderson was responsible, he was going down, along with anyone who may have helped him. Paisley deserved justice, and she deserved the truth about her death to come out.

Emily reached for the files and perused them. "This isn't enough to prove anything. Where's the recorded tape of McElroy? All I see is his written statement. I know he gave an oral statement, because I witnessed it."

She scrolled through other papers. Information about McElroy's death. It appeared George was trying to prove it was a homicide. There were papers with names of officials, businessmen and even law enforcement agents, as well as the ME in Austin who might be on the take due to missing files, photos and other evidence that mysteriously vanished. The list was fairly exhaustive.

"He was making a case," Stone said.

Emily nodded and shoved the papers back in the folder and then into her large handbag. She picked up the bowling ball and frowned.

"What is it?" Stone asked.

"Ball feels lighter than it should. You not notice that?"

"Not really."

"Well, I used to bowl."

New fact. Stone filed it away. She laid the ball on the bed and then put her fingers in the three holes and grinned.

"You sly ole man, George." She pointed at the holes. "There's a mechanism in here. I feel it. Needs to be pushed." She did so, and the bowling ball unlatched. It had been weighted enough to fool the common person but also had a hollow compartment to hide things. Emily pulled out a USB flash drive. "That's going to have Gil's recorded statement. There will be no second-guessing that it's his voice. Unlike the written statement."

"Let's get his laptop too. It was in his office on his desk. We might find something hidden in there as well."

Emily placed the bowling ball back into the bag, then returned it to the closet where she found it.

Stone started down the hall, Emily following. As he turned the corner into the living room, she let out a bloodcurdling cry.

FIVE

Stone whipped around. Emily had been disarmed, and a man clad in black, including a mask that covered his face, had a chokehold on her, a glinting knife at her neck.

"Toss your gun or I slice her open," he said, his tone menacing and gravelly.

Stone took half a second to gauge the situation. The attacker had come in silent, got the jump on Emily. Stone figured he meant what he said. He'd cut her neck.

If Stone didn't drop the gun, Emily had no hope. But if he did toss it, then they'd both end up dead. No way Stone could reach her before the man cut her, and he probably had a gun too, though he'd chosen not to use it. Probably knew Emily had a better shot of disarming him if he used the gun. Going for a blade this size would cut her hands to shreds.

"Don't make me say it again." He pressed the

tip of the blade into Emily's soft flesh, and she winced but didn't cry out. A dot of blood colored her pale skin.

Stone had no choice. With one hand raised, he slowly squatted and laid his piece on the hardwood, then gently slid the gun across the floor.

"On your belly. Hands behind your back," the attacker commanded like someone who knew the ropes. Was he in law enforcement?

"You don't have to do this," Stone said.

"Don't bother with the meager negotiation skills you've been trained with, Texas Ranger. It won't work. Just keep your mouth shut, do what I say, and maybe I'll let y'all live."

Y'all. Local accent. He hung on to that fact. This guy had a knife to Emily's throat, and the man in the camera who was dressed exactly the same had made an air slice across his throat as a death threat. He'd lain in wait outside, knowing Stone and Emily would clear the house, then he slipped inside while they were in another room.

But Stone wasn't a rookie, and if the media got wind of a former Texas Ranger and an active Texas Ranger being murdered inside the home of the recently deceased director of the PIU, they'd have that splashed on every channel and all over the internet. Feds would descend. The governor wouldn't want that kind of attention. He couldn't pay off every single person in law enforcement. This guy had to know that too. So what was his plan?

He pressed the tip even farther into Emily's neck, and she did cry out this time.

Stone's heart raced, and he obeyed and lay flat on his belly, his hands behind his back.

"Drop your handbag, honey."

She did as she was told.

The man did a quick pat down and chuckled. "Nice try." He pulled the flash drive from her pocket and shoved it inside his own.

Making eye contact with Emily, Stone spotted fear but also calm determination. She was going to make a move. "I'm doing as you say. Just don't hurt her."

"Keep your fat mouth shut."

Emily grabbed her attacker's right arm, holding the knife with her other hand, then twisted, sliding under his arm and wrenching it around his back, forcing him to release the knife. "I don't think anyone is going anywhere," she said.

Stone jumped to his feet, but the black-clad man was lightning fast, kicking her knee and sending her to the floor.

Stone lunged toward him.

The man snatched her bag and raced down the hall.

"Go! Go!" Emily hollered, and Stone hurdled her and gave chase.

As he approached George's office, the man was already diving out the window with the laptop in hand. Stone followed suit and pursued him.

The man jumped the privacy fence and Stone did the same. He chased him down the sidewalk, behind a neighbor's house and then through another backyard into a densely wooded area.

The assailant's clothing morphed into shadows. Without a gun, Stone knew continuing the pursuit would be foolish. He doubled back and called out as he entered George's home to let Emily know not to shoot.

"In here," she said.

He found her at the kitchen table with a bag of frozen peas on her knee. "I got cocky," she said through a sigh.

"Maybe a little." He winked and sat across from her. "How bad's that knee?"

"Well, it ain't great. But I don't think he tore or dislocated anything. So there's that."

They sat in silence for a few moments before Stone finally spoke. "He took our evidence. We got nothing."

She groaned as she stood. "Don't remind me. My knee's going to be bruised, but I can walk. Let's not stick around any longer."

Stone huffed. "He knew we'd show up here after what you saw on your security camera. So he didn't toss the place but lay in wait nearby. I'm not sure if he came inside planning to kill us or hoping you'd know where George kept his files. Maybe both."

"Yeah. Cocky and stupid working for me tonight." She groaned. "Let's be smarter next time."

"You were smart. You made some good moves, Ranger."

"Yeah, well the only move I have now is a limp."

Stone helped her out of the house, and they hobbled back to his vehicle in silence. Inside his truck, he locked the doors and turned to her. "Whatcha thinkin'?"

"Probably the same as you. This guy has a background in law enforcement. Maybe someone in private security. Local. Strong and smart, maybe a little cocky too. But definitely smart. He couldn't kill us. He knew that by the way he was positioning us. I imagine he was hoping we wouldn't be as smart too, but at least in that case, we were." She sat quietly, her finger to her lips. "From the voice, I don't think it was Paul Henderson. Can't say it wasn't someone he hired though. Probably was."

"But we aren't ruling out Paul personally killing our victims?"

"No. He could have been the one to kill them,

but it's possible he had someone else do the dirty work—keep the blood off his hands. I do think whoever attacked us tonight was the same person who killed Ranger McElroy and George."

They couldn't be certain. Not yet. But Stone's gut said the same thing.

Now that they were certain these deaths were no accident, Stone had to break the news to his mother. His stomach clenched at the thought. He'd rather think about the case. "Do you think the killer will back off now that he has Gil's information?"

Stone met Emily's wary gaze. "No. I think he'll tie up loose ends."

"Yeah," she said breathlessly. "That's what I thought too. I'm a loose end. So are you."

"And who knows. There might be someone else out there who has information worth murdering over."

There would be more spilled blood.

Emily gripped Sissy's shoulders with tenderness and confidence. Stone's sister had been stewing about this lunch since she set it up. Sissy had never worn a recording device before. She wasn't law enforcement or used to being undercover. But today was her lunch with Martin Landers, the chief of staff for the governor.

He might have inside information, and Sissy

was going to try to coax it out of him. She had been anxious and rightly so. Emily wanted to help ease her nerves and make her feel comfortable. If she went in nervous and jittery, Martin would recognize it. He'd known Sissy for many years.

"It's one lunch with a friend. You've known him since college. Been to his home to eat a meal, and you are friends with his wife. You have no reason to be nervous. Besides, you've made it abundantly clear that you do not believe he's involved or privy to the governor's nefarious doings."

Sissy tucked her long black hair behind her ears and nodded as she released a pent-up breath. "I know. But this feels wrong. My palms are sweaty with guilt."

Emily grinned and straightened the small locket on Sissy's neck. Inside was a tiny recorder. "I understand. It feels deceitful, but we need to know if he's complicit. These women deserve justice. Your sister deserves justice. Do this for Paisley."

"I know. I am. But even if he's not complicit, he won't own up to even suspecting a hint of malice on behalf of the governor. Martin is a private person and he's ambitious. He won't be taken down with the governor, even if he knows Paul's committing homicide or having homicide committed."

That would make things difficult.

Sissy fidgeted with the locket and Emily put her hand over hers. "You can't mess with this. Unless it's your normal behavior to fool with your necklaces." When Sissy put her hand down, Emily continued, "Time changes people. Maybe he's not the same success-thirsty man he was when you knew him in college."

"You're right about time changing a person. I changed a lot after Todd died."

Emily's heart broke for the young widow. She couldn't imagine losing the love of her life. If she ever had a love of her life. Losing her dad had been devastating enough. Even more so after the truth bomb dropped about his secret family.

"I'm sorry. I can't imagine losing a husband, but I lost my dad. And things changed. Things came to light…"

"What kinds of things, if you don't mind me asking?"

She did. But it might calm Sissy's nerves, and Emily needed the woman smooth and on her game. "He had a secret family." She shared the story in a nutshell and realized it had relieved some of her own anxiousness and stress.

"I'm sorry. We can talk about it more later if you'd like. I'm here to help."

Emily sure could use some. "I appreciate that. If we get time." She straightened her shoulders and gave Sissy another appraising glance. Dressed in a red flowy shirt and boot-cut jeans with red cowgirl boots, she was a vision. A stunner. "You look great. Just be you."

"Me with a recording device like a noose around my neck. This little thing feels like a five hundred–pound weight." She smiled, but Emily caught the wobble in her voice.

A heavy knock came on Emily's bedroom door.

"That'll be Stone. It's open," Emily called.

Stone stepped inside and cleared his throat. "Ready?"

Sissy nodded.

"We'll be listening. Just do what you do best. Create a conversation and environment that gets him talking. Pretend he's a patient." He nodded and abruptly left the room.

"He's not much of a hand-holder," Sissy said and strode toward the door. Emily didn't fully agree. Stone had been a huge source of emotional support for her and most definitely a handholder, but she didn't want to admit that to Sissy. The last thing she needed was Stone's sister believing Emily had romantic feelings toward her brother. She did not. But she couldn't deny she wished she'd said yes to the tacos and guac those years ago. He'd been a colleague though, and she had strict rules on not dating them. Truth be told, he was a colleague now too.

There would be no romantic notions taking up homestead in Emily's heart.

Sissy drove separately to the restaurant while Stone and Emily followed at a good distance in case they were being tailed. Emily knew a good tail could fool even the best trained professionals, which did not sit well with her. She kept alert and checked the mirrors frequently.

The vehicles split as they made their way into the downtown district. She and Stone would circle around while Sissy went straight to the restaurant's parking lot. After two circles, they parked in the public lot and hoofed it.

"Is Sissy going to be cool?" Emily asked.

"I hope so." He plugged his ear with a small earwig and gave one to Emily. She stuck it in her right ear and let her hair fall over it. "We're ready, Sissy."

"I just walked in," she whispered. "I see him. He's at a table near the back by the bar."

"Okay, we'll be right outside and listening. If things get hinky, just say, 'I miss the college days,' and we'll get you out. Be cool."

"Right," she whispered, and the sounds of clanking silverware, glasses and voices in the background filtered through the tiny speakers.

They muted their mics so Sissy wouldn't hear

or be distracted by their conversation. Then Stone tugged her arm. "Let's duck in the coffee shop next door."

"I could use a coffee. I didn't sleep much last night." Emily had tossed and turned, and her dreams had been invaded by the shadowy man with the knife to her throat. She instinctively touched her neck where he'd drawn blood, the sting still present.

Stone's expression turned grim as he glanced at her throat. She adjusted her collar to hide the bright red mark. "He's gonna pay for that," he said with quiet fury.

"He's going to pay for a lot." If they could find him.

Once inside the café, she ordered a peppermint mocha—'tis the season—and Stone ordered an Americano while they listened as Sissy and Martin made pleasantries and talked about some old times, then caught up on Sissy's life and work. She sounded calm and more herself than earlier. After finishing their coffee, Emily said, "I want to go inside the restaurant and see Martin Landers's face as he talks with Sissy."

Stone adjusted his earwig. "It's a risk though. Martin knows me."

"Everything we're doing is a risk. We'll be careful. I promise."

Stone nodded. "Let's go." As they approached

the restaurant, Sissy and Martin were discussing Talia, his wife, and her interior design business and volunteer work with Janice Barr-Pemberton's nonprofit organization Green House. They helped women out of abuse, trafficking and domestic violence. Getting them homes, education and jobs. Every year, they held a large gala around Christmastime to raise funds, and the Brighton family hosted it at their ranch. Talia was on the fundraising and gala committee.

"I do hope you and your family will come again this year," Martin said as Stone and Emily entered the restaurant. "Talia would love to see you. She was just talking about you the other day."

"I'm sure we will. I don't know any event quite like the Boots and Christmas Bow Tie Gala. It'll be sad without Tiffany there this year. She loved helping with that event. Paisley always did too."

Nice segue into Tiffany. But Emily bristled internally. The Spencer family was deeply connected to these people and their lives.

Emily and Stone found a table behind a half brick wall, allowing a partial view of Martin and Sissy but concealing them. Martin was a tall, lean, fit man. Probably a runner. His blond hair grayed slightly at the temples. His nose was a bit hawkish and his dark blue eyes round and spaced widely on his face, but it worked for him.

Martin and Sissy ordered their lunch and when the server left, Martin sighed. "I was shocked about Tiffany's death. She'd just had brunch with Talia to discuss the gala. Gave no hint, no indication she was contemplating suicide or even depressed. It makes no sense."

"No, it doesn't." Sissy leaned in. "Makes me wonder if it wasn't suicide after all. You know, I never thought Paisley would take her life by suicide either." She left it hanging.

"I never thought that either. But what are you saying? Someone killed Tiffany? Maybe Paisley too? Wouldn't the authorities know that?"

Sissy waved her hand at the seemingly ridiculous idea. "I know. It's absurd but still. I do wonder. What if their deaths weren't suicides, Martin?"

Martin looked from right to left and bent toward Sissy. "It's not absurd, but it is far-fetched. It would take a lot of power to pull that off. Cops. Coroners. Maybe even family. I don't know. But I will tell you one thing. The day before Tiffany died, she had an argument with Paul. She'd been vocal about her stance on the environment. Wanted him to pass the upcoming bill for stricter environmental laws. But he wasn't going to. I guess he finally told her so."

"And you think that argument got her killed?"

Martin's eyes grew wide. "Because of Paul?"

He laughed. "No way. I think she went home and told her husband she'd had it out with the governor of our good state, and that went over like a lead balloon. Paul mentioned talking to Judge that night. Didn't say what about. But Talia said that Judge and Tiffany argued often, mostly because Tiffany wouldn't fall in line with Judge's political views."

Hearing that, Stone leaned in close to Emily. "We need to check that," he whispered.

"Judge Williford may have had motive to kill his wife, but why the other women?" Emily asked.

"I don't know," Stone said.

Then they went quiet as the conversation continued in their ears.

"Well," Sissy said, "if the cops get wind that Tiffany's death might not be suicide, they'll be asking anyone within a week's time frame where they were the night Tiffany died." She sipped her water with lime.

For being nervous, Sissy was doing a bang-up job at leading Martin where she wanted him to go.

"Well, we don't have to worry. Unless you don't have an alibi." He chuckled. "If not, you can say you were with me and Talia that night at our house."

"You were at home on a Saturday night? I find that hard to believe," she said.

"Well, for once we were. Hey, Sissy, don't be sharing that thought with too many people, okay? If it gets around that you're implicating Judge, it could get ugly for you and even worse if you're implicating Paul. He's the governor and your family's friend. Yeah?"

"Yeah. I just… I guess I just don't want to believe Paisley ended her own life. I don't want to believe someone else did either."

He reached for her hand. "I know. It's been rough. Especially on you."

As their lunch was delivered and Sissy and Martin began eating, Emily took a moment to evaluate what she'd heard. Martin's alibi was being home all night with his wife. They needed to corroborate that. Tiffany had died sometime before 7:00 a.m. and after midnight, according to a friend who saw her leaving a restaurant at about 11:30 p.m.

"We need the autopsy report, even if it is doctored," she whispered to Stone. "But to ask for it means we're investigating. And I trust no one to ask."

"I trust my cousin, Dom DeMarco. He's the Cedar Springs detective looking for the vanished crime scene photos from Tiffany Williford's death."

Emily didn't want to get into the trust argument again. Blood meant nothing. "Maybe. But we could use this Boots and Christmas Bow Tie Gala to snoop around. Investigate informally."

"Whoever is behind this already knows we're investigating. If you're there, he'll know why you're there."

Fair enough. "I still say we go."

"Oh, definitely," he said with a grin. "Just know we're not being inconspicuous. At least to him."

"Yeah, but I don't want the media getting wind of it either. We stay discreet." Emily watched Sissy and Martin as their conversation resumed on a casual note. She didn't like Martin Landers.

He gave her a bad vibe.

Stone peered out the kitchen window, coffee in hand. He hoped the gray sky this morning wasn't an indication of the upcoming day's investigation. The clouds rolled and grew fat like fluffy balls of dust announcing an angry storm to come. He checked the weather app. Sure enough, storms were rolling in later this morning like chaff in the desert.

After lunch yesterday, Stone and his brothers had been called to an accidental shooting. A hunter had been cleaning a rifle, and it had fired. That had taken the rest of his and his brothers' afternoon. Sissy had been on-site to offer grief counseling services if the family wanted to retain her.

They had.

She'd spent some of the afternoon with the two junior high children left behind. Stone had never been one to numb to tragedy, death and loss. While they cleaned up the remnants, he spent the time praying for the family. Prayer mattered. It had been the prayers, support and love from his church family that had gotten him and his family through Dad's and Paisley's deaths. There'd been no judgment or ill will about Pai's eternal resting place due to the manner of her death. Kindness and compassion had been a banner over their home and God's love a shield.

Before Stone had drifted into fitful sleep, he'd remembered them once more in prayer.

Today, Sissy was there again with her two therapy cavaliers. Stone had risen early to work on the ranch with Bridge and Rhode, who had been distant this morning.

Stone couldn't be sure if it was due to the fact that Rhode and Emily had never made their mistrust right. Rhode could hold a grudge, and it appeared Emily might carry one as well. Stone had noticed Emily's mistrust was next level and maybe borderline paranoia, but her job had no doubt shaped her cynical view. Day in and day out, she dealt with corruption and deception in people who had committed to serve the people of the great state of Texas.

He wasn't sure what had shaped her ideas in her personal life. Could be what drove her to want to work in the Public Integrity Unit. She wasn't exactly an open book, but Stone would like to know her better, what made her tick. What would garner a yes to tacos and guac? He finished the dregs of his coffee, then rinsed the cup and placed it in the dishwasher. Mama wasn't up yet, which was odd for her. She'd always been a before-dawn riser. It was her best time of day to have quiet time with her Bible. Not a day went by for Stone in his growing-up years that he didn't see Mama or Daddy in their Word, usually with a cup of coffee beside them.

"Penny for your thoughts."

He startled and grinned at Mama in the doorway. She wore her robe, and pillow creases ran down her cheeks. "I was thinking, it's kind of late for you to be sleeping."

She patted his shoulder as she passed him on her way to the coffeepot. "I didn't sleep well last night. It happens as you age. So I decided to sleep a little later. Is that a crime?" she asked with light teasing and sipped her coffee.

"Just unlike you."

"You worry too much."

Probably true. Definitely true. But Mama and the family—the ranch—it was all on his shoulders now since Dad had passed. It weighed heavy.

Emily entered the room. Dressed in jeans and a long-sleeve white shirt that had been tucked in. "I heard stirring downstairs. Figured everyone was up by now. May I?" she asked and pointed to the coffee.

Mama chuckled. "You are welcome here, and that means you're welcome to anything we have. Food. Drink. Horses even. You don't need to ask."

Emily's cheeks reddened, and she nodded her gratitude, then poured a cup of coffee and added sugar and a heavy splash of cream. "What would you like to do first today, Stone? I know you have an opinion."

"I know you do too. And mine won't matter if it doesn't line up with yours."

"You got that right, Ranger."

He caught the playfulness in her eyes, and her voice held a hint of flirtatiousness, which squeezed his chest. He decided a half cup more wouldn't hurt, and he retrieved a new mug. "I was thinking I—or we—should go visit Janice Barr-Pemberton. She was Tiffany's friend and might know what her meeting with the governor was about. Tiffany may have confided the details of her and the governor's argument or even more personal information concerning her marriage to Judge."

Emily nodded but said nothing. Mama was still in the room, and Stone had been pondering how to tell her that Paisley's death had been a homicide. Neither manner of death would bring solace. Pai was still gone either way. But the guilt they all carried on some level—of not seeing signs or asking the right questions or not paying attention—could be laid to rest. Finally.

Still. Now wasn't the time.

Mama put a piece of toast in the toaster. "I was thinking we'd put the tree up tonight. I know we usually do it on Christmas Eve, but I got an invitation to the grand opening of the old zoo for that night. I thought it might be fun and different."

"What's the old zoo?" Emily asked, clearly intrigued. "When I was a little girl, I loved the zoo. I wanted to be a lion keeper."

Lion keeper? Emily was a lion. Fierce and sleek. No fear. "I loved the monkeys," Stone said.

"Because you and your siblings acted like them," Mama interjected and snickered. "Always pranking one another or wrestling. Climbing trees and giving me heart palpitations."

"That's what kids are for," Stone said. Then he turned to Emily. "Anyway, back in the early 1920s, they built a zoo, but after a bear was poi-

soned and a lion died, it kind of went kaput.
Anyway, time and nature did its thing, eroding
enclosures and growing up around it. The historical society decided to make it a landmark,
and they've been working with the parks and
recreation crew to turn it into a park with hiking paths and an event venue. All the proceeds
go back into the historical preservation funds."

"The soft opening is Christmas Eve for business people, politicians—"

"Fancy pants people of Texas who have
money," Emily said.

Mama laughed. "Yes. And us. We have family connections from Reed's fraternity. But
we've never been 'fancy pants people' as you
call them."

"Sounds fun," Emily said. Yeah. And it sounded
even more like an opportunity for Emily to investigate.

"Yeah, Mama. We can do our Christmas Eve
tradition tonight," said Stone. "I doubt anyone
will mind. I'll swing by the tree lot and get a
tree later."

"Perfect."

Stone put his second dirty cup into the dishwasher and kissed his mama's head. "Be back
later."

Emily followed him outside, and they drove to
Janice Barr-Pemberton's. She kept an office for

her nonprofit in downtown Austin, but she spent most of her time in a restored Colonial deep in the Texas hills. Secluded and private, it was what many of the women she helped requested or felt more comfortable with, as many of them were running from abusers and bad men.

The curves were sharp and the inclines steep as they drove into the Hill Country. "I love this area," Stone said.

"Yes, it's gorgeous compared to the desert. I like both."

After they descended a large hill, the white Colonial came into view. A beacon of hope. Green House was a place for renewal. Fresh starts. Green with new life. They paused at the iron gates, and Stone showed his driver's license to the guard.

"Do you have an appointment?" the security guard asked.

"No, but I know Janice personally, and this is Texas Ranger Emily O'Connell." No point hiding that fact and it might get them onto the property faster than his creds of being an old family friend. Emily showed her Texas Ranger star, and the security guard nodded and let them pass.

Inside the house, they were greeted by a woman with a pert nose and wary eyes. She led them to Janice's office at the back of the home. The scent of pine and cloves swirled in the office, and Janice greeted Stone with a peck to each cheek.

"How's your family?" she asked and offered them a seat and coffee, which they declined.

"Well." He introduced Emily and they made small talk about family, business and how Green House was doing.

"Always looking for more donations. I hope the gala is a big hit this year." Janice crossed her legs. She was tall and slender and dressed in a black pantsuit that matched her hair and eyes. Janice had always been an attractive woman, even now as she pushed into her sixties.

"We'd like to talk to you about Tiffany Williford," Stone said.

"Oh, Tiff." Her eyes welled with tears. "I just can't wrap my brain around it."

Emily handed her a box of tissues from the desk, and Janice plucked one, then dabbed her eyes. "Did Tiffany confide in you?" Emily asked.

"Of course she did. We were friends. But I can tell you right now that Judge would never in a million years have killed her. I know you're with the PIU. Why else would you be here?"

Emily refrained from redirecting her line of thinking. Stone figured she'd let Janice believe what she wanted to. "They argued often. Do you know why?"

"Because Judge married a woman far younger

than himself and couldn't keep up. He was a golf-playing, cigar-smoking, lounge-by-the-pool-on-Sundays kind of man. Tiff loved to travel. She had causes she believed in. She wanted to see change. Judge used to be that way once. I think it's part of why Tiffany fell in love with him."

"Is that what she argued with Governor Henderson about—one of her causes? We heard they got into it, and we also know that the governor called Judge Williford not long after Tiffany came to see him. She confide any of that?"

"No. Well, she did want Paul to sign the environmental bill she'd been lobbying for. I suppose they could have argued over that. Paul wasn't going to sign it though. Royce told me—"

"Told you what?" A voice carried through the room and Royce Pemberton II entered. Tall and imposing but with gentle eyes. He grinned, his dimple creasing. "My ears were burning," he teased, then he caught sight of Emily. "I don't believe we've had the pleasure. Royce Pemberton."

Emily stood and shook his hand. "No, but I do know you, sir. Chair of the Texas Ethics Commission." Stone heard the admiration in her voice. Honesty and integrity meant everything to her. Didn't need for her to say it to see it.

"Indeed, and you are?"

"Texas Ranger Emily O'Connell, sir."

He grinned again. "Impressive. What branch?"

"PIU."

His eyes narrowed as he seemed to contemplate why Emily would be here.

"Just asking some questions," Emily said warmly.

"I see." He shook Stone's hand. "Hope to see you at the gala. How's your mother?"

Stone went through the small-talk spiel and Emily used the time to hand Janice a card and to tell her to call if she thought of anything else. They let themselves out and got inside Stone's truck. Emily turned on the radio once he cranked the engine. "I'm a music-on kind of person."

"I see that."

"What do you think?" Emily asked.

"About music?" he teased.

"About our meeting."

"I think Janice has no idea about Paul. And I'd like to know what she was about to say Royce had told her before he entered the room."

"Perfect timing too."

They rounded hills and curves, discussing ideas and theories. The truth was they had nothing new. They were only filling the silence. As they rounded a bend, a black truck came out of nowhere, which wouldn't be that big of a deal, but it was gaining on them.

Faster.

Stone pressed down the gas pedal. "Not to scare you, but you might need to hang on."

"What? Why?" Emily glanced in the side-view mirror. "Stone, that truck—" The rest of her sentence was cut off as the oversize truck rammed into them full force.

SIX

Emily's body lurched forward, her seat belt slicing into her skin, the burn intense. The truck rammed them again and she gasped for breath, her body jarring. Stone's hands were white-knuckled against the steering wheel, his jaw set and his eyes laser-focused on keeping them on the road.

Up ahead loomed a vast lake.

It didn't take Emily but a second to figure out the driver's goal. Stone swerved, the smell of rubber filled the air, and smoke rose around them from the friction. Her blood pumped fast, whooshing in her ears.

"If I can dodge him until we get past the lake, we might be able to outrun him or…" He was clearly thinking of a way out of this.

The truck was huge with a lot of horsepower, and Stone's work truck was old and not in any shape to combat the big engine revving behind them.

Maybe she could help. She pulled her gun, but Stone's voice cut her off. "Don't!"

She looked at him. "I can shoot out his tires. Get him off us. Maybe wreck and arrest him."

"If he rams us while you're unbuckled, you'll go straight through the windshield. And you can't get a good shot buckled up. So just sit tight. Please," he said through gritted teeth.

"Silent Night" began to play.

Holy night...

The truck rammed them again.

All is calm...

They spun toward the lake, as Stone fought to regain control. Emily cried out as one more solid ram sent them airborne.

Stone cried out to God as they hit the dark waters with a bone-jarring thud. Emily's head snapped back, nailing the leather seat with a force that sent stars dancing in her head.

"Stone, we have to move. Fast."

But Stone didn't answer.

His head was resting against the wheel, a trickle of blood running down the side of his face. Emily's heart froze.

Water began seeping into the truck. She undid her seat belt. If she rolled down the windows, water would flood in too fast. If she was alone, she could swim out, but she had Stone to think about, and the weight of the water against the door kept her from opening it.

She'd have to wait until they were fully submerged for the pressure to equalize and open the door.

The truck continued its nose-dive into the depth of the murky lake.

She pressed the release to unbuckle Stone, but it was stuck. Panic enveloped her. This was only supposed to happen in movies, not real life!

Sunlight slipped away as they sank. Dark. Eerie. No sound outside the cab.

Water was at their seats. She opened the glove box. No knife.

Sleep in heavenly peace...

The radio signal silenced. Frigid water rose to her neck, and she tried not to panic. Once the truck was fully submerged, she could open the door and get out, but she had to free Stone first.

Emily pulled and yanked on the seat belt to no avail.

She laid Stone back against the seat to keep water from his face. The gash was deep. He'd need stitches.

If they survived.

She prayed and forced herself to calm down.

Now the water was up to her chin and Stone's neck. She kept her head tilted back, breathing deeply, trying not to go into hysterics.

The water was cold. Quiet. Powerful.

The thought came to her suddenly. Most men carried pocketknives. To check his pockets, she had to bend forward, her head going under as she shoved her hand into his right pocket.

Nothing.

She came up for air, sucked it in and then reached over and tried the left pocket.

Bingo.

Once again coming up for air, she crouched on the seat, her nose only inches from the roof. She inhaled deeply, fearing for Stone, who was now completely enveloped by the lake water.

Time was running out.

She opened the pocketknife and cut him free.

Then she attempted to open his door, but she couldn't get it open. It was supposed to open now that the pressure had equalized. Fear gripped her heart and her lungs begged for air. She turned and felt around to find her own door handle, but it wouldn't open either.

Oh, God! she silently cried out.

Stone was underwater. Passed out.

Dying!

With trembling hands, she went for her gun, her lungs on fire and her brain reinforcing her need for oxygen.

Her chest grew tighter and tighter. She aimed and fired, the windshield spider-webbing.

Black dots spotted her vision.

Her brain screamed for air.

She kicked against the windshield. Nothing. Kicked again.

Finally the windshield gave way into the darkness. She grabbed Stone and hauled him from the truck, thankful for weightlessness underwater.

She swam upward, but she was exhausted.

The dots turned into waves of blackness.

She was going to pass out.

There was no light above. They were down deep. Too deep. She'd never make it.

But she had to. Fighting the burning and desperate need to inhale, she kicked until she could see light. She was close to the surface.

Just a little farther.

Tired. So tired.

Finally, her head broke through the water and she gulped in sweet air as she raised Stone's head up. She sucked in, the burning even sharper though the dots cleared. They weren't too far from land, but the exhaustion was overwhelming. She tucked Stone under her arm like she'd learned in junior lifeguard class and worked with all her might and muscle and prayer to get them to shore.

Once she made it, she had no time to lie there

and breathe or rest. She checked Stone's pulse. She couldn't feel one.

Trembling, she began compressions.

One and two and three and four and...

Another round.

Another. "Don't you even think about dying on me, you bullheaded pig!"

One more cycle, then he coughed and gagged. She rolled him to his side, and water spewed out as he continued coughing, gasping and gagging. But it sounded like precious music to her ears. And she praised God he was alive.

Finally, he rolled onto his back, staring up at her. He blinked several times, his eyes rolling back in his head, and then he murmured, "I love you," and passed out again. She checked to make sure he was breathing and then ran up the hill, her clothes heavy and clinging to her. Her socks were squishy in her boots.

Once she reached the top, she saw nothing but isolation and seclusion. Their phones were underwater. She could hike back to Green House, but she didn't want to leave Stone alone. He needed medical attention. She probably did too, but for now, adrenaline kept her pain-free and kicking.

She trotted down the road, hoping to find help and not encounter the black truck again, but the driver had accomplished his plan and was probably long gone, thinking he'd get his payday now.

Who would have known they were at Janice's? They hadn't been followed. Or had they? The only people who knew was Stone's family.

Bridge, Sissy.

Rhode.

A pit formed in her gut. Had she made a mistake in trusting them? The sound of a car coming closer sent her darting to the side of the road in a defensive crouch.

Not the black truck but a black sleek sedan.

She recognized the driver.

Janice Barr-Pemberton.

Emily flagged her down and Janice skidded to a stop, rolling down her window. "What on earth?" She hurried to Emily, concern filling her dark eyes. "What happened? Where is Stone?" Her voice wobbled. "Oh, no, where is Stone?" she said again with more force.

"He's okay. He's at the bottom of the hill and needs an ambulance. We had a car accident."

Janice's hands shook as she retrieved her cell phone from the car and called 911.

"You stay up here. Point the way for the first responders," Emily told her. "I'm going to go back down there with him. I don't want to leave him alone."

"A car accident? I saw skid marks on the road.

Was that you? What actually happened, Ranger O'Connell?"

"Someone tried to run us into the lake and succeeded. That's all I'm at liberty to say."

"It's about Tiff, isn't it? She was murdered, wasn't she?" Her voice cracked.

"Stay here." That was all Emily would say. She rushed down the hill, nearly tumbling until she reached Stone, who was now sitting up and rubbing his head.

"Don't. You might have a concussion. You've got a bad gash." But he was sitting up and alive, and now she could breathe easier and think about what he'd said before he'd blacked out the second time.

I love you.

The words twisted her gut in a way she'd never felt before. Other than her father and grandfathers, no other man had ever spoken those words to her. Not that Stone knew what he was saying. He was out of his gourd.

Still.

Instead of meditating on it, she explained what happened after they hit the water and rebuked him three more times for trying to stand. Finally, the ambulance showed up, and the emergency personnel did their initial assessment, then tried to put Stone on a backboard and carry him. That did not go over, and he climbed up the hill beside her. Right as they clambered inside the ambulance, she grinned and nudged him.

"Just so you know, you told me you loved me right before you passed out a second time."

He smirked and pointed to his head. "I have a concussion."

"I thought you were hardheaded," she countered.

He snorted. "True. But if I can't remember it, then it didn't happen. I think I'd know if I told you something like that. Are you trying to get a steak and fancy dessert out of me?"

His playful teasing through a weak voice sent her heart skittering. "I see you've upped your game. Last time it was tacos and guac." She arched an eyebrow, waiting for an equally snarky retort.

"You remember that?"

"Which time?" She laughed. "You asked me twice."

"You like making me squirm, don't you?" His grin rippled through her veins like a flight of fireflies glowing in a meadow. "Have you no mercy? I almost died."

She did in fact like making him squirm. Loved bantering with him. It was easy and comfortable, as if they'd done it their whole lives. "PS, I almost died too. And I saved your life."

"Thus, steak and not tacos. But to be fair, you

did use my pocketknife to cut me free, and since it's an extension of me, then technically I saved my own life. You know, 'cause of the knife."

She contained her cackle. "You'd make a great attorney, Harvey Specter."

"I've heard that before. *Suits* reference is new." He waggled his eyebrows and closed his eyes. He was masking his pain with the flirty banter. He needed rest, so she let it drop, and they rode the rest of the way in comfortable silence.

When the ambulance parked under the hospital awning, the paramedics jumped out and moved Stone to a wheelchair, which he protested in vain. He peered back as they began wheeling him inside. "Hey, Em?"

"Yeah?"

"Did you say you loved me back?" He chuckled, as they moved behind the doors where she couldn't follow.

No, she hadn't said it.

However, something was brewing in her heart. Something she did not want.

And couldn't seem to control.

"This is unnecessary," Rhode said as Stone poured the water into the reservoir under the Christmas tree.

"Mama wants to do our Christmas tradition tonight. We're doing it tonight." Stone had taken six stitches to the head, downed way more ibuprofen than one should and was working hard to ignore the soreness and pain radiating through his body. After leaving the hospital, he'd met up with Bridge, who had gotten the blue spruce at the Christmas lot since Stone had been a little busy almost dying. Due to wooziness and not wanting to go to the hospital again, Stone had Bridge bring down the ornaments from the attic.

All he wanted was rest, but he was going to make this night special for Mama even if she had told him to bow out. They would decorate the tree and bake cookies—at least his mom and Sissy would bake—then they would watch *A Christmas Carol*. Rhode preferred the Jim Carrey animated version, but they never wavered from the version Mama loved best. The 1951 adaptation with Alastair Sim as Ebenezer Scrooge.

Rhode persisted. "You have a minor concussion. Not to mention someone has tried to kill you repeatedly. Christmas tradition can wait, bro. Mama said it was fine."

Except it couldn't wait. Something in his gut gnawed at him. They needed this. The family. Even Emily. Though she was upstairs and had been for the past three hours. Hopefully, she was getting the sleep she needed. The woman had saved his life. He owed her so much more than a night of holiday festivities. He'd omitted to

Mama that he'd been knocked unconscious. No point scaring her any more than he already had.

He noticed she wasn't downstairs getting cookie dough ready either. Maybe the bad news had zapped the energy out of her.

"It can't, Rhode. We have other events coming up, and tonight is the best night. You and Bridge can take the lion's share of decorating the tree and stringing the lights. I'll keep my feet up most of the evening and be in charge of the music playlist."

Rhode ran his hand through his hair, which had grown out considerably since his detective days with Cedar Springs PD. His long locks fell right back over his eyes. "How long are you going to let your hair grow?"

"I don't know," he said, irritated. "What's that got to do with tonight?"

"Nothing." Stone shrugged and stared at the undecorated tree. "It's crooked."

Rhode groaned and worked on straightening it. "You're too much of a perfectionist."

"And you're not nearly enough of one." He carried the pitcher back to the kitchen. Sissy entered. "Hey."

"Hey," she said. "I'm gonna get the cookie dough made and put it in the fridge for later. Mama's pretty tired. I fear all this stress is weighing on her. She's a worrier. Like you."

"I'm not a worrier."

Sissy cocked her head.

"I mean not about unnecessary things."

"'Be anxious for nothing,' so sayeth the Word of God." Sissy grinned and began getting out the ingredients for Mama's secret family recipe sugar cookie dough. She wouldn't even give it to her best friend. That's how secret it was.

Lady and Louis sat by the island awaiting a little morsel of something. Sissy grinned, opened the freezer and gave them each a blueberry. Their tails wagged and they settled under the kitchen table.

"How's Emily?" she asked.

"I haven't seen her since we got home from the hospital."

"I hear she saved your life. Bridge told me."

"She did. She's a fighter." And feisty and flirty and fun and a woman of faith.

Sissy measured the wet ingredients in one bowl. "That she is." Raising her eyebrows, she tossed him a knowing smirk.

"Nothing is going on." Granted, he'd told her loved her, but he legit didn't remember saying it. It wasn't true. But he did like her a lot. More than he probably should. She'd turned him down twice already, and she had trust issues, and he had a mountain of things to be concerned about. A relationship wasn't on his list. No more room.

The Chipmunks' Christmas album suddenly belted from the living room. Stone groaned.

Sissy frowned. "I thought you were going to take charge of music."

"I was. I am." He strode from the kitchen into the living room, where Rhode stood with a grin on his face, singing along in his best Chipmunk voice.

Stone chuckled, then weakly hollered, "Alvin!"

Instead of cutting the song, he let it play. They needed silliness and laughter tonight. And Rhode had been uptight since Emily had joined their family ranks. To see him laughing and smiling meant everything. Stone did not need him getting low on life and spiraling—again.

Bridge waved from the window and came inside. "Really? *A Chipmunk's Christmas*?" He held up a bottle of sparkling cider.

"Yes, and you're Theodore," Rhode said. "I noticed a few extra holiday pounds around your middle." Rhode kept a straight face, but Stone had to cover his mouth until Bridge's glare sent him and Rhode into spasms of laughter.

Bridge was merciless at the gym, and any accusation that he wasn't cut grated his nerves. So they'd taken to calling him fluffy and soft every chance they got.

"Ha. Ha. Johnny Depp in the early 2000s called. He wants his hair back," Bridge retorted.

Rhode patted his abs. "He want his six-pack back too?"

Bridge had been shaking the cider bottle and popped the cork, spraying it all over Rhode, hitting Stone too. Rhode hunched like a football player and tackled Bridge in good fun, sending them both crashing to the hardwood floor.

Emily entered the living room. "Do you always kick off Christmas tree night with a round of wrestling?"

"Nah, we just call that Tuesday," Stone said.

"If you weren't half dead, bro, I'd have you down here with us," Bridge said as Alvin and the Chipmunks belted "Santa Claus Is Comin' to Town."

When a truce had been called, they cleaned up the sticky cider mess, and Mama entered the living room looking rested. "I see I've missed some of the party."

"We're saving the best for last." Stone hugged her.

Sissy entered, wiping her hands on her apron. "Dough is in the fridge. Let's decorate."

Rhode grabbed a strand of lights and went to work while Bridge sorted through holiday knick-knacks.

Emily leaned in. "Don't you think you should be resting, Stone?"

"My dad used to say he would rest when he

was dead. I'm adopting it. And anyway, Rhode is messing up the Christmas lights. Let's take charge."

"I doubt he'd appreciate me taking over his job." Emily raised an eyebrow.

"He'll get over it." Stone stepped in. "Okay, me and Em are taking over the lights. This looks…well, not even close to perfection."

Rhode rolled his eyes and glanced at Emily. "You a perfectionist too?"

"I'm a precisist."

"Is that a word?" he asked as his eyebrows knit.

"It is when it comes to the lights." She smiled and it reached her eyes. She was trying, and Stone admired that. Would Rhode?

Rhode held her gaze a beat, then two. Chuckling, he swept his hand out for them to be his guest and take over. "Well, by all means let's be precise when it comes to Christmas lights and crime investigation." He winked and she nodded.

"Hear, hear. Let's drink the cider to that. In this case, maybe *lick* the cider might be more apropos." She lifted her shoe from the hardwood, the squeak of sticky residue resounding.

"Guess I wasn't that precise in cleaning." Rhode's smirk was the kind that won women's hearts, one that Stone envied. Not because he wanted to win hearts, but Rhode always got the girl he was eyeing. And while he was only making nice with Emily, he was still oozing charm Stone never had. He kind of preferred Rhode acting Grinch-like around Emily.

"Isn't that *your* job? Cleaning?" she deadpanned.

Emily fit into their sarcastic family well. Too well.

She handed Stone a strand of lights. "Can we show them how it's done?"

He cleared his parched throat. "Yeah. Yeah, we can."

They took over and rhythmically partnered as if they'd been stringing Christmas lights together for decades. Afterward, everyone joined in the decorating using Mama's treasured ornaments. Many of them had been made during their school years. Beads, handprints, pictures like the one Rhode held. Sissy's handprint turned into a reindeer with her first grade school photo pasted in the middle.

Rhode held it above Sissy's head. "Hey, it's a picture of Thithy! My twin thithter."

Sissy jumped, attempting to swipe it from Rhode, but he had several inches on her. "Give that to me!"

When she'd lost her two front teeth, they'd constantly made her say words with *S* to hear her little lisp. Partly to tease but mostly because it was pretty cute, and getting scolded by Mama and Daddy had been worth it. They'd always doted on their baby sis, the youngest of the Spencers by three whole minutes.

"You're the betht twin thithter in the whole world," Rhode said through more laughter.

"Shut up," Sissy said. "I was adorable."

"*Was* is the keyword," Rhode added. No one gave Sissy a harder time than Rhode. But they had a bond that was undeniable. One even Stone and Bridge couldn't break through or cross.

"Har har." Sissy gave up on retrieving the decoration and looked at Emily. "Dough is ready. You want to help me and Mama? Get away from these stinky boys for a while?"

"They do stink." Emily patted Stone's shoulder and followed Sissy into the kitchen.

Bridge smelled his pits and shrugged, and Rhode shook his head.

"All right, let's get this done. I'm tired," Stone said. They got to work finishing the tree and wrapping the banister in garland, then placing Christmas blankets and throw pillows on the couch and every chair in the house, it seemed. "I don't get why a woman needs so many blankets and pillows."

Bridge rolled his eyes. "It's a girl thing. If it's soft and warm and cute, they're havin' it. Wendy had nine thousand—" He broke off. "It's a girl thing," he said abruptly. "I'm gonna check and see if we missed any boxes in the attic."

Stone gave Rhode a knowing look. "Been awhile since I heard that name roll off his tongue."

Wendy had been out of Bridge's life for two years. Stone wondered if their breakup had anything to do with his leaving the FBI. He wouldn't talk about his former fiancée or why he left a job he loved.

"Yeah. But it's Christmas and we both know it's hard for him. What kind of woman leaves you a breakup note on Christmas then vanishes? Literally."

"The kind in the CIA who knows how to disappear."

"The tree looks spectacular," Mama said, cutting off their conversation. "Gift time."

Stone settled on the couch—too sore and tired to gather around the tree—but the others sat on the floor eagerly awaiting gifts like they were three-year-olds and not ranging from early to late thirties. Tradition called for one gift on Christmas Eve, and since they were doing their Eve celebration a few nights earlier, gifts were to be had.

Emily hung back.

The smell of vanilla and sugar and Christmas filled the air.

"Emily, you have a goodie too." Mama motioned for her to sit with Rhode and Sissy.

Emily's smile faltered. "I do?"

"Well, of course, hon. Come on. Join the family." Mama looked around. "Where's Bridge?"

"He's in the attic. I'll get him," Rhode said and walked to the stairs. "Briiiidge!" he hollered at the top of his lungs. "Present tiiiiime!"

"I could have done that, Rhode," Mama said dryly.

Rhode shot her a proud grin, footfalls sounded on the stairs, then Bridge appeared. Some of the light dimmed in his eyes, but he sat beside Rhode. Emily chose a chair near Stone, too sore to get down on the floor too. Sissy's dogs nestled beside her.

"Each of you is a gift to me, even you, Emily. It's been refreshing to have another female in the home, and your presence is pure joy."

Rhode grunted and Bridge elbowed him. Stone shot him a dirty look.

"I love y'all so much. And I can't imagine Christmas without each of you." Her eyes shone with tears. "Now to the gifts."

She handed them out, all wrapped in pretty paper with matching tags and bows. Stone was careful to open his while Rhode ripped into his without any thought. Emily hadn't touched hers yet.

Stone and the boys received new Stetsons and pajama pants with Santa hats and cowboy boots.

"You don't...want us to wear these simultaneously, do you, Mama?" Rhode cautiously asked with a hint of mischief curling his lips. "I feel like that belongs in a calendar of some kind."

Sissy giggled, and Bridge covered his face with his hat to hide his amusement.

"No, Rhode," Mama scolded.

Sissy nudged Emily. "Let's open ours together."

She nodded and they unwrapped their bulky packages. Sissy had a Cavalier King Charles throw pillow and a red Christmas blanket with snow globes.

Emily removed a throw pillow showing two vintage Smith & Wesson pistols. She grinned. "I love this."

Stone chuckled.

"I thought you might," his mama said. "You're a tough cookie."

"Speaking of cookies, I need to check on them," Sissy said and darted into the kitchen.

Emily removed her other gift. A deep blue blanket with snowflakes and red Christmas bows. "Thank you so much, Marisol. These are wonderful, and I'm stunned you even thought of me."

"You're part of our family." She cast a quick

glance at Stone and his gut tightened. *What exactly does that mean?*

"Cookies are cool. Let's ice them, then get on with the movie!" Sissy called from the kitchen.

As Stone stood, the doorbell rang. Who on earth would be here on a Tuesday night? Dread filled his gut. "Y'all go on. I got this." He headed for the front door and opened it.

Great. There went the holiday spirit.

SEVEN

Emily couldn't believe that she'd been included in the gift giving and that in such a short time, Marisol Spencer had picked a gift that was truly Emily. She loved the throw pillow with the guns. Christmas had been a lot of fun each year, but less fun the years her father was "traveling"— meaning visiting with his other family. That thought tempted to sour the mood, but she refused to let it. Tonight had been special and fun.

During the years it had only been her and Mom, they'd made cookies, usually premade dough from the refrigerated section at the grocery store and a plastic container of icing, but they'd played Christmas music and laughed, and on Christmas Eve they baked a cake to celebrate the birth of Jesus. Mom had taught her that Christmas had much more meaning than gifts, parties and Santa Claus. They'd attended church after icing the cake—on the years that Dad was out of town anyway. Then after the lovely candlelight service, they had come home and lit the birthday candle. Blew it out and sang "Happy Birthday" to Jesus and had cake.

On years Dad was home, they'd watch all the Christmas cartoons like *Rudolph the Red-Nosed Reindeer* and *Santa Claus Is Coming to Town*. And the one with the mouse who jacked up the clock that sang a Christmas song to Santa, so his father had to fix it. Dad had said he'd always be there to help Emily fix any problem.

But he'd only created massive ones.

Emily shook off the thoughts and watched as Bridge and Rhode wolfed down cookies and milk, and Sissy gave the dogs little doggie cookies. A big family would have been a lot of fun. She was enjoying their intimacy, even when they were wrestling on the floor over shaken up sparkling cider.

The smell of popcorn filled the air. Emily wasn't sure she had room to put another bite in her mouth. She'd eaten four Christmas cookies. Soft and flaky like little cakes instead of crunchy cookies. Addictive and, oh, so delish.

"Emily, did y'all have any traditions in your family?" Sissy asked.

She shared the ones she'd been thinking about just minutes earlier.

"I love that idea of baking a cake. We should do that Christmas Eve morning and, when we get back from the event at the old zoo, eat a piece of cake," Marisol said. "Sound good?"

Rhode grinned. "Ma, you had me at *cake*."

"Same," Bridge said. "What kind of cake?"

"It's cake, bro. Does it matter?" Rhode asked and snagged yet another cookie. He'd eaten more than he'd iced.

Bridge ignored him. "I vote yellow cake with fudge icing." He licked blue icing off his finger. "What kind did you bake?"

"White with white icing," Emily replied. "I guess because Christmas is about purity and snow…in most places. Definitely not here."

"Definitely not. Although we've had snow less than a handful of times." Bridge stood and washed his hands as the sound of voices came into the kitchen.

Emily bristled. She'd recognize the man beside Stone anywhere. Not only did he have a connection to the governor and the victims, which put him on her radar, but Beau Brighton was in the tabloids, in *People Magazine*, on TV and all over social media sites. He was tall, rugged and carried the reputation of a bad boy. He and his family owned a dude ranch nearby, but from what Emily had heard, Beau Brighton did more jet-setting and partying than helping his family, including his older sister, Coco, run the ranch.

"Everybody," Stone said, trying to get their attention.

Rhode jumped up. "Bruh. Where've you been? I tried calling. Can't text a man back?" He gave Beau a manly hug. Drawn in with a handshake then a quick slap on the back with the other hand.

Sissy looked up and her back stiffened.

"Hey, Sissy."

"Beauregard," she said coolly and his jaw twitched. "What are you doing here?"

"I just got back in town. Been to Vegas."

"You win?" Rhode asked.

Beau's full lips turned south. "Not even. But it was fun. Thought I'd come by and catch up. Answer your texts in person. I didn't realize a party was going on."

Marisol glanced at Sissy, then smiled at Beau. "We're doing our Christmas Eve tradition tonight since the zoo event is on actual Christmas Eve."

"Oh, right. I think Coco mentioned that. I don't want to impose," he said, but Emily didn't see Beau Brighton feeling bad about showing up where he shouldn't be.

"Nonsense. We're about to watch *A Christmas Carol*. You in?" Rhode asked. "And we have Mama's secret recipe cookies."

Sissy shot Rhode a look, and he returned it with a scowl.

"I love these things." Beau snagged one. "But," he added as he looked at Sissy and held her gaze with his intense blue eyes, "I probably ought to go. Thanks for the offer," he said to Marisol, then cast his sight back to Sissy, and Emily caught a flicker of pain in his eyes. "You look good," he murmured.

Sissy didn't respond.

"Where's your family, Beau?" Marisol interjected before the room became too tense.

"Oh, Monaco. Coco's with Keifer. Skiing in Aspen and staying through Christmas. So it's just me and Netflix." He laughed softly, but Emily recognized the loneliness in his tone.

Marisol exchanged another look with Sissy. Clearly there was bad blood between those two. Sissy sighed. "No point going home to a dark house. Might as well stay and watch the movie."

"Really?" he asked softly.

"Whatever." She blew through the room. Marisol followed.

Finally, Beau seemed to realize Emily was in the room. "You're new."

Stone introduced her as Emily O'Connell. Probably to remind her tonight was an off-duty night. No Texas Ranger, just Emily. She kind of liked being introduced this way. But she also wanted to ask him about Tiffany Williford. However, this was family night, and it would only bring up sorrowful memories of their sister Paisley. She decided to wait.

Beau shook her hand. "Nice to meet you." Polite enough. No flirt. From the rumors, he pretty much flirted with anyone who had two X chromosomes.

"In all seriousness, is she coming back?" Beau pointed toward the doorway where Sissy had exited.

"Yeah," Rhode said. "Just maybe don't sit next to her if you value your parts."

Beau chuckled and snagged two more cookies. "What are we watching again?"

"*A Christmas Carol*," Stone said and escorted Emily into the living room with a bowl of popcorn. They took the love seat while the others took the couch. Sissy and Marisol returned and nestled in the recliners.

Once popcorn and cookies were distributed, they began the movie. Toward the end, Rhode's phone rang and he excused himself. Bridge fell asleep, his mouth open. Beau chucked popcorn into it, most of the kernels landing on Bridge's chest.

Sissy hid a snicker. As if laughing at Beau's antics might be crossing some kind of invisible line.

Marisol also dozed, but no one messed with her. Rhode entered again.

"Hot chick?" Beau asked.

Rhode only grinned. "I could ask you the same. Who you been texting all night?"

"Shh. It's the best part. Ebenezer's life has changed for the good. Some of you might take a lesson," Sissy said sharply.

"Ouch," Beau whispered. "You've always been brutally honest and I stress *brutal*."

"Yeah, well, you're just stress. Now shut up."

"Yes, ma'am," he said through a lopsided grin.

Emily loved this part in the movie too. Tiny Tim would be saved from a suffering death. And Ebenezer learned he had to change. Had to learn to love. To be loved. That family was important. She felt her phone in her pocket like a concrete block reminding her that she had unresolved family issues too. Was she being a scrooge by not taking Dottie's phone calls?

"So I hear there's an investigation about Tiffany's suicide," Beau said as the credits rolled, Marisol and Bridge still slumbering.

Emily perked up. "Where did you hear that?"

Beau stood and stretched. "I know people. I was just curious."

"We don't know much," Rhode offered.

Emily's blood boiled. He was clearly giving away they were investigating.

"Judge hire you?" Beau asked.

Stone stood. "If someone did, you and Rhode

both know he's not at liberty to disclose that."
He eyed his PI brother, his jaw tight.

"He'll just text him the minute we walk out of
the room. Like I'm about to do right now." Emily
strode for the door.

"I'll go with you," Sissy said and followed her.

"Neither of you need to be outside at night taking a breather or a walk or whatever," Stone said.

Emily shot him a defiant look, then blew out
the back door, Sissy right behind. She wasn't
going to wander into the pastures or the driveway or the road. "No offense, but I do not trust
your twin."

Sissy sighed. "He wouldn't have spilled anything more. But I understand your need to keep
things quiet."

Emily disagreed. Rhode was pretty much
about to spill the tea. He was good friends with
Beau. "Is it normal for Beau to pop in like this?"
Maybe he had known who she was and that she
was here. He'd have to. Whoever told him would
have filled him in that a woman Texas Ranger
with Stone was asking questions. Why not tell
her earlier he knew who she was?

"Not really. Not anymore. He probably didn't
realize I was here." Sissy folded her arms over
her chest as they meandered from the deck. "Is
this safe?"

"Honestly? I don't know. But I need air. You

should probably go back inside though. I won't be long or go far."

The night was crisp and the moon full, but she could see so many stars out here in the night sky. If she weren't so mad, she'd enjoy the gorgeous view.

Sissy ignored her. "Beau used to come over all the time. Especially around the holidays. His parents traveled often and left him and Coco on their own. I think he was lonely. They didn't have family events like we did. Hired help did all the decorating, and caterers brought in gourmet snacks, desserts and dinners." She shrugged. "He's probably feeling it again now."

"Did you two have a thing?"

"I don't want to talk about that. I'm better at talking about you." She grinned and looped an arm through Emily's.

"I like you. I don't like a lot of people," Emily said and laughed.

"I like you too. Maybe you and Stone can get together, and I can have a sister…again," she whispered and Emily held her closer to her.

"I'm so sorry about Paisley."

"I know. Me too."

"As far as Stone goes, we're colleagues only. But we can be friends." She could use a friend.

"I'd like that."

They walked in comfortable silence. Emily

wondered if this was the kind of night when the Savior was born. Silent night. Holy. Peaceful.

A thundering crack split the sky and Sissy cried out.

Emily threw her to the ground as another bullet hit the dirt next to her foot.

But Emily wasn't worried about herself.

It was the blood seeping from Sissy's shoulder. She'd been hit.

The *pop, pop, pop* sent Stone snatching his gun from the side table and rushing outside, his brothers right behind him.

It was unmistakable gunfire. He'd warned them not to go out there but hadn't pushed it. Fear raced through his veins.

He could hear Rhode telling Beau to get back inside the house.

Another round of fire pierced the night sky and then more gunfire close by.

"Sniper," Bridge said. "Gunfire is far out and up close. Two shooters?"

Stone could care less where the shots originated. He cared more about the target.

Emily.

Another louder shot fired. "No. It's Emily. She's got her gun." She was returning fire.

"Get down and fan out," he called to his brothers, but they were already on it. "Emily! Where are you?" He wasn't sure how far out toward the pasture she was, and the thought of her without cover—and Sissy too—made his blood freeze in his veins. He prayed and waited.

"Marco," she called quietly enough he could hear, but not a sniper out in the woods like they suspected. Stone marveled at her insight. Calling out her exact location would reach the shooter's ears too. He was stupid to even ask, but his rational thought was out the window at the moment.

"Polo!" he called back and lay flat on his belly, army crawling in her direction.

Another bullet fired, spraying dirt nearby.

He continued his crawl. "Marco!"

"Polo," she said. From the sound of her voice, he knew he was close.

Once more a bullet fired from the east side of the property, but no bullet hit. One of his brothers must be firing on the shooter. Maybe even caught him.

Silence hung in the air. Only his breathing and slithering along the ground reached his ears. "Marco," he called out quieter.

"Polo."

There in the distance about six feet away were two shadowy figures. Emily and Sissy. "I see you," he whispered.

"Sissy's been hit, Stone."

Stone's world slanted as he picked up his pace

and finally reached Emily and his sister. Emily was shielding Sissy in a protective manner, and Sissy was lying still. Too still.

"Sis?"

"Hey, big brother. I'm fine." But her voice was weak and trembled.

"She took a shot to the shoulder. We need an ambulance. She's losing blood." Emily held her even closer. "But it's okay, Sissy. You're going to be just fine."

"Approaching," Bridge called out. "Don't shoot." He darted next to Sissy. "She's hit." Fear laced his voice, and he pulled his cell phone and called 911.

"Where's Rhode?" Stone asked.

"He went on the east side of the property. That's where the shots were coming from. Looks like only one shooter. I'm going to see about Mama and keep her calm." He bolted into action.

Stone held Sissy's hand but looked at Emily. "Can you tell me what happened? Did you see anything?"

Emily shook her head. "We were leisurely strolling when the first shot was fired. We ducked for cover, but Sissy was already hit. We didn't hear anything. It was peaceful. I'm sorry. I should have listened to you. Not been stupid and prideful and angry. Sissy, please forgive me."

"You didn't make me come out here, Emily.

You told me to go back inside. Nothing to—" she winced "—forgive."

Finally, sirens screeched, growing louder as they drew nearer. Red and blue lights flashed. Cedar Springs PD and the paramedics were here.

First responders did their job, and as they loaded up Sissy in the ambulance, Beau rushed outside. "Sissy! Is she okay? Where is she?"

"Calm down," Stone said. "She's going to be fine." The paramedics told them it looked like a clean through-and-through, but they couldn't be sure.

"And don't go to the hospital, Beau," Bridge said with a curt tone as he stepped toward them. "Sissy wouldn't want you there, and the media tends to follow you. We don't need any of that surrounding us. Rhode can keep you updated."

"Where is Rhode?"

"Right here," he said, shoving his phone in his pocket as he neared. Sweat dotted his brow and his jaw was clenched. "I lost the shooter in the woods. Sorry."

"It happens," Stone said, but he was irritated. "Let's get to the hospital." Emily had ridden with Sissy. She'd insisted on going and Sissy hadn't said no. She guessed they'd formed some kind of sisterhood. He'd formed some kind of bond with Emily too, but he didn't know how to define it or if he even wanted to or could. But it was there.

Like kudzu. Growing. Entangling and overtaking everything it came near.

Like his heart.

Sissy was released four hours before dawn. The paramedics had been right; it had been a clean shot. After cleaning and stitching and prescribing pain meds, they'd sent her home with orders for rest and physical therapy to come. Stone was just happy she was alive and well.

While in the waiting room at the hospital, Stone had talked to Emily about launching an official investigation into Tiffany's death and a formal inquiry to see the crime scene photos. It was time to apply some pressure, he'd told her. The media might not have wind of an investigation into the governor, but he knew. A hit man had proven it more than once.

Bridge had interrupted the conversation to inform them that his contact had called regarding the bomb that had exploded Stone's truck. While the device was somewhat similar to those used by the at-large bomber Kerry Von Meter, there had been too many differences to be linked to him. Bridge had also thrown out Martin Landers as a suspect, proposing he was somehow framing the governor. Stone was glad it had come from Bridge and not himself. Emily had her eyes on Paul Henderson and no one else, because Texas

Ranger McElroy had thought it was the governor and evidence supported it. But someone close to him who had power and access could have been setting him up. It was plausible, and Stone didn't want Emily to have tunnel vision, but he also didn't want her to think he and his brothers were trying to shift the focus from the governor due to their personal connections.

Emily had taken it well and calmly without throwing out accusations. But she'd still asked for more time. Once they went to the governor, the media would be alerted. If it wasn't Paul Henderson, his reputation could be damaged. Stone and his brothers had agreed.

But besides talk about the case, Stone had noticed Emily checking her phone, scowling and ignoring it as if she had unwanted calls or texts. He'd asked her if everything was okay, and she'd said yes, but he had a feeling she wasn't being forthcoming, but he let it drop.

Now, as Stone sipped a cup of cold coffee, he relished in the silence of the house. Mama was resting in her room and Bridge had gone to his cabin to get some sleep. Rhode was with Beau, who hadn't listened and had come to the hospital anyway. But at least he'd had the sense to drive Rhode's car to keep the media away. Once he'd learned Sissy would be fine and would be released, he'd left with the request no one tell

Sissy he'd even been there, because she would just be angry.

Beau had been right, so they'd agreed.

The doctor had said Sissy would likely sleep most of the day but to wake her for pain meds to stay ahead of the pain. Stone had sent Mama on to bed with the promise he'd keep Sissy dosed. He'd set an alarm on his phone to remind him. With so much on his plate, he didn't want it to slip his mind. He was stressed to the max and feeling it. A little dizziness, light-headedness. His skin flushed hot.

Drinking a fourth cup of coffee with all the caffeine probably wasn't helping, but he was exhausted and sore and unable to go to bed. Yawning, he sprawled out on the couch, hoping for rest, but doubting it would come.

Emily entered, her red hair up in a messy bun. A baggy sweatshirt hung on her slender frame, and she wore leggings, no socks or shoes. She was a stunner even with the shadowy moons forming under her eyes.

"You guarding the house?" She nestled on the other end of the couch and draped the Christmas blanket Mama had given her last night over her feet.

"I can't sleep. What about you?"

"Nope. We're in a game of cat and mouse, Stone. If I don't catch the killer, he will most certainly catch me. And he's a big fat cat. I'm just a wee mouse. I'm being brave, but the longer this goes on and the more the attempts on my life escalate—and the fact that we can't find any solid evidence or trust anyone if we did have it—well, I'm kind of freaking out."

Stone sat up, put his coffee on the coffee table and held her chilly hands in his. "Come here," he whispered and pulled her across the couch and into his arms. He butted his back against the couch cushions to make room for her. Then he fixed the Christmas blanket to cover her back up.

With her nestled against him, it felt right. Peaceful. Safe. "I know it's scary. But we will figure this out." Her hair tickled his nose. "And we'll find out who is doing this. I'll keep you safe." After last night, he'd done a lot of thinking, and he'd made a phone call to a friend who owned a security company. "A security team is coming out later today to install a state-of-the-art security system and put some lights outside and motions sensors." It was going to deplete a lot of his savings, which he'd been hoping to sink into the repairs of the ranch, but his family's lives came first. They'd figure out the livelihood later.

"You don't have to do that for me." Her fingers slipped between his, and she squeezed his hand.

"I'm doing it for all of us. After today, this

place will be a straightjacket even Houdini couldn't escape from." He smirked. "Our next step is going to the gala tonight."

"The Boots and Christmas Bow Tie Gala?"

"Mmm-hmm." He felt his eyes growing heavier. How strange that holding Emily batted away all the anxious thoughts and filled him with solace. He rested his chin on her head and closed his eyes. "All the players will be there. Martin Landers. Paul Henderson. Judge Williford, I presume. Plus friends and acquaintances of our victims, including my sister. Maybe we'll catch a break."

"I'm tired. Maybe we can catch some sleep now."

Or maybe they'd catch their death.

EIGHT

Stone frowned at himself in the mirror. Penguin suits. Not his cup of tea. He didn't even care for cups of tea too much unless he was sick with a sore throat. But they needed to be at this event. He peered closer in the mirror. At least the bags under his eyes were gone. He and Emily had innocently fallen asleep on the couch, and he had to admit it was the best sleep he'd had in months. Until his alarm went off to wake Sissy and give her pain meds.

He'd managed to slip off the couch without waking Emily. After that, he made some calls, showered and fed Sissy's dogs. Finally, Emily had woken, and a tiny veil of awkward tension had dropped. While nothing romantic had gone on, the intimacy of napping on the couch together had created an awareness that, for him, had always been there but concealed. Now, it was out there.

Emily must have felt it too.

A soft knock drew his attention away from his thoughts. "Come in."

Mama entered wearing her robe and house slippers, a cup of flowery-smelling tea in hand. "You look dapper."

"This bow tie is crooked. I hate it." He growled as she approached and set her china cup and saucer on his dresser. "I have always and will always hate these events. We're not some highfalutin people, Mama. If it wasn't for Daddy being in a fraternity with Paul, they wouldn't give us a second glance."

Mama sighed and went to work retying his Christmas bow tie. Same one he wore every year. Red with fancy white lettering spelling out *Merry Christmas*. "Maybe. Maybe not. But stop judging people because they have money."

She had a point. She always did.

"Mama, I have to tell you something." He had to tell her. Now. If they did question the governor and it came out what the investigation was about…then he'd rather Mama hear it from him than the news or a reporter calling her. "You need to sit down for this."

Her eyes held questions, but she listened and perched on the edge of his bed as he told her the truth about Paisley's death and exactly who they were investigating and why.

Mama sat stunned, and then her face crumpled and sobs erupted from deep in her throat. Stone held her tight, rocking her as she had done for him when he was a boy and had skinned his knee or fallen off a horse. Both had needed her love and warmth. "I can't believe it. Are you sure?"

"We're sure it's a homicide, but we have no definitive proof it's Paul."

"It can't be, Stone." She looked up through red-rimmed eyes. "Paul is a kind man. He has his sins and he will answer for them, but he was good to your father. I wasn't going to tell you this, but he offered to help your father six months before he passed—again. The first time was about ten years ago, and your father accepted the help both times."

What? He'd taken the money? His stomach turned to lead. Did this mean Paul thought he had the Spencer family in his pocket? "I knew it had been offered but he said no Spencer man was taking a handout."

"Of course he said that. And he wanted to do it on his own, but he was going to lose everything. He settled for losing his pride only."

Stone wished he'd have known. Maybe somehow he could have helped.

"I loved your dad, but he wasn't the best with finances. I just don't see how a man who had been like a brother to your father and given him money with no strings attached could have murdered or had your sister killed?"

"Mama, people who do vile things can also do good things too. Actions don't reveal motives."

"That's true." She patted his cheek. "Can we keep this between us?"

"Of course. I can stay home if you like." He needed to be with Emily and work the investigation, but his mama needed him too.

"No. You go. I'd rather be alone anyway, and Sissy will likely sleep. Besides, I imagine that gorgeous redhead looks even swankier than you tonight."

"She's not a fan of swanky."

"Well, you're even more of a match than I originally thought." She closed the door behind her before he could protest his feelings about Emily. He pocketed his wallet and strapped on his ankle piece, then left his room. As he passed the stairs, a flash of emerald green caught his eye, and he did a double take.

He peered up as Emily descended the stairs. Fiery red hair with strawberry blond highlights hung in soft waves down her shoulders and the long green gown was silky and moved with her soft curves. She lifted the bottom of her dress, and he spotted her ankle holster and laughed. "Not every girl accessorizes so well, huh?"

Oh, it was working for him.

"Sissy loaned me the dress a couple days ago. I didn't have anything, and she told me it was ludicrous to buy or rent one when she had plenty. Guess y'all attend these types of affairs often."

For a moment, his mouth wouldn't work. His throat was desert dry and his brain a swampy marsh. The words were stuck.

"Stone?"

"Yeah. No. I mean… You look incredible, and the gun is even better than your pearl earrings."

"My gun is pearl handled."

"It is?"

"No," she said and turned her nose up. "What do you think this is? An Agatha Christie novel?"

"I've never read her. But I have seen *Murder She Wrote*," he said with a grin.

She shook her head and stopped on the bottom stair, eye level with him, and his heart pounded. "I don't know if I should be impressed or be concerned."

"When in doubt, be both."

Snickering, she messed with his bow tie as if it were crooked. But Mama had fixed it. So, did she simply want to be near him, touch him? "I…" She waved off what she was about to say. "Never mind."

"No, what?" he asked, taking her hand and inhaling her soft, flowery scent.

She searched his eyes. "I just wanted to say

thank you for the nap. I haven't been able to sleep well, and…" Her cheeks turned a sweet shade of rose.

"I haven't slept that good either," he admitted.

"I felt…" She grazed her bottom lip with her teeth, and he thought he might faint onto the floor. "Safe."

He cupped her cheek, felt the warmth there. "Yeah."

One beat passed. Two.

Then throwing caution to the wind and following instinct, he moved in until his lips barely met hers.

"Mama? Stone?" Sissy called through a thick, groggy voice. "Stone?"

The almost kiss broke, and as much as he loved his baby sister, she had the worst timing ever. "Hold that thought," he said.

She grinned. "We really ought to be going after you see to Sissy."

Unfortunately she was right. "Guess so." After getting Sissy a glass of water and handing her the TV remote, he escorted Emily to Mama's car since he was zero for two on trucks. He and Emily had gotten new phones since the lake incident, but as far as going out and buying a new truck without the insurance kicking in yet, he was going to have to suffice with borrowing a vehicle.

The trip to Brighton Ranch where the gala was held was uneventful, and he was thankful for that, but he caught Emily on more than one occasion checking the rearview and tensing when a car approached. Now, they made their way up the curvy paved road leading to the Brighton's mansion. A valet took the car and drove away.

"I don't like that," Emily said. "What if someone plants a bomb again and we don't hear the click?"

"Unlikely, since the valet has to go get the car and start the engine before us." Besides, it would be too public tonight for that, and if for one minute Stone thought a valet was in harm's way, he'd never have let him have the vehicle. He held out his arm to Emily and she slipped hers through his.

"How gallant of you."

"I'm a gallant guy," he teased as they ascended the steps to the front doors of the mansion.

"My apartment can fit on this porch alone," she muttered as they entered. Servers were dressed in black with white aprons and carrying silver trays of hors d'oeuvres and champagne. "You come here often?" Emily asked, declining food and drink.

Stone snapped up a canapé. "You trying to pick me up, O'Connell?" Her comment sounded like one from an old black-and-white movie.

Something Marlon Brando might have used on a dame—and succeeded. Not that he'd use the word *dame* in front of Emily. He'd wind up picking his teeth up off the floor. The woman was tougher than rawhide, and he loved that about her. But tonight, in that dress with her hair all loose, shiny and flowing, she appeared fragile and delicate. Which was deceiving, because she could probably kick someone's backside with just the sole of her high heels.

"Pick you up? Nah, I can't really bench press more than two-forty," she sassed with a straight face as they sailed through the room, which smelled like Christmas and money.

Stone did laugh then. She had the best comebacks.

Martin Landers stood near the massive Christmas tree, which was decked in crystal ornaments and white lights. Next to him was his wife, Talia, and Governor Paul Henderson and his wife and son, PJ. He spotted Stone and raised a glass in salutation, which drew his father's attention.

The governor's gaze lasered in on Stone and then Emily. Stone noticed the quick admiration in his eyes before he excused himself and headed their way.

"Well, it's not taking long to get his attention, is it?" Emily said.

"No, ma'am, it is not. Play it cool."

She ignored him, which didn't give him much solace that she would.

"Stone," Paul said with a warm voice. "It's so good to see you."

Stone shook Paul's hand and tried to contain his anger. This man might have murdered his sister. But this man also gave his family money to stay on the ranch. "How are you?" Stone asked. "This is my date. Emily O'Connell." Better to set the tone as friendly than bring up she was a Texas Ranger, but he likely already knew that, even if he'd played dumb. Paul Henderson was no idiot.

Emily didn't miss a beat and leaned into Stone, then held out her hand.

Paul shook it. "Nice to meet you," he said. "I imagine Marisol is thrilled. She's been trying to get all you boys to settle down."

"It's a pleasure to meet you, Governor."

"Pleasure is all mine," said the hound dog. This guy might not be a killer but he was an A-one bonafide jerk. Gift giver or not. And if he'd cheat on his wife, he'd cheat in other things too.

"Well, hello again," Royce Pemberton said as he and his wife, Janice Barr-Pemberton, approached. "How are you both feeling?"

"Feeling? You been sick?" Paul asked.

"No, they were run off the road leaving Janice's nonprofit. Right into the lake," Royce said. "This extraordinary woman rescued Stone from drowning. I am honored to be in your presence, Ranger O'Connell." He dipped his chin in respect, and Emily's cheeks turned as red as her hair.

"Really?" Paul asked with what seemed genuine surprise. But he was a politician, and sometimes they put on better performances than actors in Hollywood. "That's amazing. Why were you run off the road, Stone? Accidental? I hope not on purpose."

"They're working Tiffany's case," Royce said.

"I'm actually on vacation." Emily's fingers dug into Stone's tux jacket. "But I would like to know how you came about such details, Mr. Pemberton."

"Oh, well, I heard about the accident from Janice when you flagged her down, but Trystan filled me in on the rest. Rhode told him. I assumed it wasn't confidential, but I've been discreet since I haven't read about the car accident in the paper or heard it on the news."

Her fingers dug in even more, and Stone was thankful it wasn't his bare skin or she might reach bone. "Oh. Well…" Stone said.

"You ever thought about working protective detail?" Paul interrupted with a wink at Emily.

Okay. That's enough of that.

"No, I like my job with the PIU. Catching those slimy, greedy state employees." She grinned but it was plastic. "So nice to meet you again." She was polite, but Stone could feel the ice in her tone. "I need to powder my nose. Please excuse me," she said sweetly.

Too sweetly.

The woman was a powder keg.

She strode through the crowd, and as the others walked away, he rubbed his temple.

His brother Bridge approached. "Just got here. I see we got all our ducks in a row."

"Rhode here yet?" Stone asked.

"Yeah. He's in their solarium."

By the bathroom.

Great.

Stone found Emily and Rhode in the corner. Rhode glaring and not backing down, and Emily with her finger in his chest.

Stone approached. "Let's bring this down a notch. Shall we?"

Emily spun around to face him. "He's leaking information. You said I could trust him. That I could trust you."

"I didn't say anything about the case he didn't already know from his mother," Rhode said. "I was bragging on your life-saving skills. You have some nerve."

"I have nerve? *I* have nerve?" Her voice grew louder and Stone firmly took her elbow.

"Let's get some air," Stone said.

She acquiesced, and they passed by the three stooges, as Stone liked to call them. Trystan Pemberton, PJ Henderson and Beau Brighton. He led Emily outside.

"You can't make a scene."

"And I can't trust your brother either! Can I even trust you?"

Emily's heart raced faster than a thorough-bred in the Kentucky Derby. She might literally be seeing red right now. The Spencer men knew this was a sensitive case and confidential. But Rhode didn't seem to care that his running off at the mouth could put them all in even greater danger.

Livid didn't begin to describe how she felt right now. She jerked her arm from Stone's grasp but continued to walk with him past the outdoor cooking station and swimming pool area and down the sidewalk that led to a fountain in the center of a small garden. Beyond that, several stables housed horses that cost more than she'd make in a lifetime.

"You can trust me, Emily," Stone said calmly, which only aggravated her more. Why wasn't he upset? Furious?

The sounds of Christmas music filtered through outdoor speakers, and lyrics of having a Merry Christmas floated on the crisp air. Nothing about this day felt merry and bright.

"Rhode didn't mean to overstep his bounds," Stone said. "He was impressed with you. You saved his big bro, and in the Spencer family, sadly but truthfully, I'm the one who has to save everybody else. I'm the one they look to for advice, counsel and a kick in the pants. Even while Dad was alive, Rhode looked up to me most. To him, I'm invincible. Therefore, you saving me is like…something out of this world."

She had noticed the way the Spencer family, including Marisol, looked to him for answers and fixes.

"Not to mention," he said, "you don't think I'm trustworthy, but just an hour or more ago, you were about to kiss me."

"I guess it was a lapse in judgment."

"The mistrust or the kiss?" he murmured.

Maybe both. If she couldn't trust him, then she shouldn't be kissing him. *Ugh.* That nap had been so good because she had felt safe and yet nagging in her brain was the thought that she had felt safe in her dad's arms once too, but he couldn't be trusted.

"Your silence says it all."

"It doesn't though." Guilt ate at her. "I'm always somewhat distrustful of people. It's my job. But lately, my life has kinda taken a turn. I'm not perfect, Stone."

His eyebrows raised. "Get out," he teased and she found a grin.

"I have a lot of family baggage."

"Yeah? Me too. I'm stressed out all the time. I even have high blood pressure because of it. I worry about our ranch finances, about my siblings and my mom."

She appreciated his vulnerability and honesty.

"My family baggage is recent, and it's really messing with my head." She shared with him the recent news concerning her father and the fact that she had a half sister who kept calling. "I should have been able to trust my dad, Stone. So, you see why I'm struggling to trust Rhode, who's a stranger, and even you. My heart says I can trust. My head says no one can be trusted."

Stone's jaw relaxed and he embraced her and she let him. "Trust God."

"Take your own counsel."

He chuckled. "Fair point. Em, you should talk to this Dottie. Are you afraid you won't like her or you will?"

That hit like a punch to the gut. What if she did like her half sister and wanted to get to know her? That would betray Mom. She hadn't even told her that Dottie had reached out. She couldn't.

"I'll think about it. I want to and I don't want to."

"And what about me? Do you want to trust me or not?"

She peered into his eyes. "I want to. I do. I'm just struggling. Please be patient."

Stone cupped her cheek. "I will. Emily, do you want to kiss me or not?"

That, she was not struggling with so much. "I definitely want to."

His lips met hers, and the softness coupled with the scrape of his scruff sent her floating and yearning for something that went beyond the physical attraction and chemistry. Stone Spencer was a place of refuge and safety. A place of commitment and transparency.

She felt it in the way he kissed. One that didn't invade, didn't use force, didn't get lost in passion, but held gentle restraint and asked for participation, partnership. The backs of her eyes burned as she stepped into him, feeling the heat break through his shirt. He slipped an arm around her waist, and his other hand slid into her hair, but he never crossed a line, pushed a boundary.

This was new. Beautiful. Extraordinary.

Slowly, reluctantly, he broke the kiss but not his embrace.

Neither said a word.

Emily didn't have the breath or the words to speak. To explain. Her emotions were tangled. She wanted that kiss. Needed it. But it had exposed a truth she'd refused to let surface.

She cared deeply about Stone.

Far more than she'd allowed herself to believe.

Noise snagged their attention. Under a hanging lamp over the stable door stood Governor Paul Henderson in a lip lock of his own.

With Talia Landers, his chief of staff's wife.

They disappeared inside and Emily gawked at Stone. "What is going on?"

Stone ground his jaw. "If Paul Henderson is having an affair with Martin Landers's wife, and Martin knows…"

"He could be framing the governor as revenge."

"Over the span of four years?"

"I've seen people set plans in motion that have taken longer than a decade. Ever heard of a long con?" It wasn't out of the realm of possibility, and if he was trying to get Paul Henderson the death penalty, then this was the way to go with hard evidence over time.

"Fair enough."

Emily, Ranger McElroy and her late boss might have had it all wrong.

"Excuse me."

Emily jerked her head as the governor's wife approached. "Have you seen Paul?"

Emily froze. She could not lie, but this would be painful and humiliating for the governor's wife. "I'm sorry, Mrs. Henderson—"

"He was with his father ten minutes ago, and now I can't find him. I have a headache and thought he might take me home."

Paul *Junior*. PJ. That's who the woman was looking for. Emily inwardly sighed with relief.

"He was with Rhode, Trystan and Beau in the solarium," Stone said.

The governor's wife smiled and glanced toward the stables as if a sixth sense drew her gaze there. "Thank you," she said softly. "It's so good to see you, Stone. Give your mother my best. And Sissy too. I heard about her misfortune. I'm not sure what case you're working," she said as she looked at Emily, "but I'm sorry it's bringing danger to you. I could get you some added security if you'd like."

"That's sweet of you, Mrs. Henderson. Really," Stone said. "But we'll be fine. I'll tell Mama you asked about her."

"And Sissy too."

"And Sissy too," he echoed.

She glanced at the stables once more, and her gaze lingered there, then she turned back to the mansion. A few steps later, she stumbled.

Stone rushed to her side. "You okay, Mrs. Henderson?"

"I get migraines. I just need to go home. Need to find PJ."

"Where is your security team? Can't they take you?" he asked.

Yeah, where is her security team?

"Oh, I get so tired of that."

"Let me help you inside." Stone glanced back at Emily, and she nodded.

They both could use a little space after that kiss. Where did they go from here? She didn't date coworkers. But that felt like a weak excuse right now.

She had so much on her emotional plate, and Stone was trying to carry the weight of his own family. The last thing she needed to do was fall for him. He'd want to carry her burden too, as if he had additional space for her problems on his shoulders.

Approaching the fountain, she sat on the bench, trying to muddle through the mess she'd just made. What were the consequences of kissing Stone going to be?

After twenty-five minutes, Stone hadn't returned. He'd either gotten caught by family friends, or he wasn't ready to face her. Either way, she was thankful for the breathing room.

A figure skulking toward the stables caught

her attention, and as she looked intently, she recognized him. Beau Brighton. Why would he be wandering out there alone? Did he know the governor and Talia were inside the first stable? If not, he was in for a shock.

Clicking of heels on the brick walkway shook her from her thoughts.

Martin Landers's wife, Talia. Wasn't she in the stable?

Emily must have missed them leaving when Mrs. Henderson approached, or they went back to the party another way. Whichever, Emily had her alone now.

She jumped up. "Mrs. Landers, I've been wanting to speak with you." She introduced herself.

"About what?" Talia asked.

Emily didn't have time to dance around. She leaned in. "About the stables and the governor."

Busted. It was all over Talia's perfectly contoured face. Her blue eyes widened. "What do you want? Money? A job?"

Nausea punched Emily's gut. "No. I want the truth about Tiffany Williford's death. Your husband says he was home all night. That you can corroborate. Is that true? And I'll take that truth for free with a side of no strings attached." Everyone wanted something for something. She wanted the truth and Talia wouldn't owe her anything in return.

Talia glared, skepticism in her eyes and then finally resignation. "Can I ask for discretion?"

"Of course." Asking was one thing. She could ask all day long.

"I can't corroborate. He wasn't home but I was. He didn't get in until the wee hours of the morning."

"Can anyone vouch that you were home prior to him?" In her line of work, no one told the truth.

Talia bit her bottom lip. "Yes, but he won't."

Emily let the words sink in. "The same person in the stable was with you at your home?"

She nodded. "Martin said he would be working late and not to wait up."

Talia clearly hadn't.

"The man in the stable—"

"Can we just call him the governor?" Emily asked.

Talia sighed. "Paul arrived around nine and was there until about 2:00 a.m. Then I went to bed."

If Talia was lying, what would her motive be other than trying to protect the man she was having an affair with?

"If the governor won't admit to being with you, how can you prove it?" Emily needed proof, or nothing would hold up in court if it came to that.

"I can't, but I'm not lying."

Emily believed her, but that wasn't enough. "Does Martin know about your affair?"

"No. No one knows."

Unless Martin knew about it and just decided to stay quiet and get even by framing the governor. Did the timeline match up? "How long has this been going on?"

Talia's cheeks reddened. "Off and on for about six years."

Paisley died four years ago. If Martin knew, it would make his revenge plan diabolical and stretched out. Emily wasn't leaning toward that motive and angle, but she wasn't ruling out Martin doing Paul's dirty work either.

"Anything else?" Talia asked.

"Maybe try not to be romantically involved with another woman's husband," she clipped.

Talia's blue eyes hardened. "Don't judge me. You have no idea what you're talking about. She knows about his indiscretions. That's the deal. She keeps the cushy life, and with that, she turns a blind eye." Her phone dinged, and she checked it and smirked. "I'm done here." She huffed. "I need to be alone."

She stalked back toward the stables.

She wouldn't be alone out there. As far as Emily knew, Beau was still out there.

Unless that text was from Beau. But why

would he be texting her? Surely, Talia wasn't having an affair with him too, was she? No, that was too ridiculous.

As she headed toward the mansion, chills rose on her arms and she surveyed the area.

Nothing.

Christmas music floated in the air, and the pool lights cast a romantic glow as she passed. But something didn't feel right.

An awareness came over her, and as she turned, something crashed against her head, then she felt hands push her.

She toppled, then plunged into the pool, the water shocking her. The glow of the lights underwater grew dimmer until darkness drowned her and she saw nothing.

NINE

Stone and Mrs. Henderson couldn't find PJ, and she'd ended up leaving with the protection detail after all. Stone had then searched for Rhode. He often ended up in trouble when he, PJ, Trystan and Beau got together, and Stone couldn't help but worry. Unfortunately, they were all missing, so he'd talked to a few of his father's old friends and, if he was being honest, kept some distance from Emily.

If he went back out there and they were alone, he didn't trust himself not to kiss her again. Their kiss had been amazing, but it had also clouded his heart. Emily had trust issues. He wouldn't be with a woman who couldn't fully trust him. Now, he needed to find her. Left to her own devices, she would likely get herself into trouble with that feisty mouth.

Which brought him back to that kiss.

Was it a mistake? He honestly had no idea.

Was he attracted to her? Yes. Was it more than physical attraction? Absolutely. Could it be something? Maybe. But the timing seemed to be all kinds of wrong.

But hopelessness sank the spark quickly. Where was she?

He retraced their steps. No Emily.

As he passed the vacant pool area, he caught a flash of green in the pool.

Her dress.

Emily's red hair sprawled across the top of the water like streaks of blood. No, it was blood!

"Emily!" He dove into the water, his heart hammering against his ribs.

Raising her head above the water, he swam to the pool steps. A couple of onlookers had arrived, passing by and hearing the commotion.

"Call 911!" he hollered and dragged Emily to the pavement. He felt for a pulse.

Nothing.

Hysteria raced cold through his veins, and he immediately began CPR. This must have been what it had felt like when she'd rescued him. A large crowd had gathered now. Bridge and Rhode raced to his side.

"What happened?" Bridge asked, but Stone ignored him, concentrating on CPR and praying he hadn't found her too late. Murmurs and whispers resounded, but Stone stayed focused on Emily.

Sirens wailed.

First responders cleared the crowd and took over CPR from Stone. Finally, Emily's body twitched, her eyes fluttered, and she rolled over and threw up. He'd never been so glad to see it. She was alive!

Sputtering and coughing, she tried to sit up, but the paramedics wanted her to lie still. They asked a series of questions.

She knew what day it was and her name and who the president was. "Someone hit me and shoved me in the pool," she said through a hoarse voice.

"You're going to need stitches," a paramedic said.

She looked up at Stone.

"Welcome to the club," he teased, but his adrenaline was still pumping with terror. She'd almost died. The thought curdled in his gut.

"You just can't handle a woman rescuing you, can ya? Gotta make it even." She smiled and winced.

He snorted and walked with them to the ambulance. "I'll be riding with her."

His brothers and PJ, Beau and Trystan followed.

"Find out what happened. Who did it," he told

his brothers. "You better bring me some solid news." With that, the doors to the ambulance closed, and they were once again on their way to the hospital.

Stone paced the ER waiting room. They'd taken her straight back, but that meant nothing. She could hole up in triage for hours. Finally, she walked out in a half-dried gown. Her hair was hanging damp and limp around her shoulders, and she had a few streaks of mascara running down her freckled cheeks, but she was alive.

"I was about to storm back there, but they wouldn't let me," he told her as he ran to her side.

"Rules are rules."

"Bah humbug."

She laughed through her nose. "I'm fine. Three stitches. Mild concussion. Script for the good stuff, and you know the drill."

He touched his own stitches. "Indeed. Someone has a serious fetish with using bodies of water in attempted murder."

"Agreed. Now to find out who did it. I'm putting money on the governor or Martin Landers. Maybe a bigger pot on him. Guess what?" she asked as he led her outside to the parking lot.

"What?"

"Talia lied for Martin. He was not home all night. While you were trying to find a lift for the governor's wife, I talked with the chief of staff's wife. Seems my knowing her little secret loosened her lips." She cradled her head in her hands. "Man, my head hurts."

She filled him in on the conversation and her accident.

"So you saw no one around."

"I didn't say that. I saw Beau Brighton go into the first stable, then a few minutes later while I was talking with Talia, she got a text and excused herself, claiming she needed to be alone. I saw her head toward the stable. Maybe it was the governor. I never saw them leave the stables."

"I did. He was inside for a while, then I lost track of him."

"So, the text could have come from Beau."

"Or she did need to be alone because you rattled her."

Emily rubbed her right eye. "We've got a web that is woven with so many secrets and lies, we may never get it untangled. But it's odd that Talia would be having an affair with the governor and Beau."

He helped her into the car, then they drove in mostly comfortable silence to the ranch. As they turned up the drive toward the house, he felt he needed to say something, anything, about that kiss. She hadn't been so concussed that she'd forgotten. But his gut twisted. What was he going to say?

Emily broke the silence. "About that kiss earlier."

Great. Now she was going to control the narrative.

"It was an incredible kiss, Stone. I mean, don't let it go to your head or anything, but the timing is all wrong. I hope it won't affect the rest of this investigation, because I actually do like working with you."

He was on the same page, but he felt the pang of disappointment anyway. "When you trust me."

"Yeah. That's part of the timing thing. Is the kiss going to affect us professionally?" she asked.

No. It'd probably mess with him personally though. "No, I'm in agreement with you." He parked and opened his door but looked at her. "And it was incredible." He held her gaze, wanting to lean in and do it again.

She scraped her top teeth over her full bottom lip as if savoring the taste again, and his gut clenched. "Well, at least we're on the same page. On another note, I would prefer your mother not know about my near-death experience tonight. We've stressed her out enough."

"Same page again," he said through a rasp.

As they entered the house, his cell phone rang, breaking the silence. "It's Bridge." He answered.

"Talia Landers was just found dead in the stables at Brighton Ranch."

Emily watched as Stone's hands balled into fists, and his jaw worked furiously.

"Okay. Hold on before you go any further. I want Emily to hear." He led her into the living room and put the phone on speaker. "We're good now."

"Talia Landers was found dead in the stables at the ranch. Martin went to look for her, and Royce Pemberton was with him when they found her in a pile of hay in one of the stalls. According to Martin, Talia loved the horses, and they often visited to ride, to get out of Austin and enjoy the air, so her being out there wasn't odd to him."

"Yeah, well, we know more, but keep going," Stone said.

"That's why he said he went out there to check."

"You there now?" Stone asked.

"Yeah. Local PD are still here too, but they're about to clear out after the ME leaves. I haven't seen her body, but from the scuttlebutt, it appears she entered a stall to pet a horse, and it got spooked. Kicked her in the head."

"Or it could be that someone made it appear

to be an accident when it wasn't." Emily's blood was boiling again. "I want on that scene."

"You could get clearance easy, but it gets worse," Bridge said.

"How?" How could it get worse?

"I went in at Mr. Brighton's authority, as a crime scene cleaner—which we'll need to handle, and he said sooner is better. Since it's not being ruled a homicide, we can have access as soon as they clear it. No other civilians were allowed in."

"Go on," Emily said.

"I found a wallet buried in a pile of hay outside the stall. It's Beau's."

Emily sat on the couch and let out a long sigh. "I saw Beau go into the stable. And not long after, Talia returned to the stables."

"Returned?" Bridge asked.

Stone filled him in on what they'd witnessed before Emily was pushed into the pool and left to die. "If Beau was at the stables, then he couldn't have been the one who attempted to kill Em."

"But he could be Talia Landers's killer," Emily said. "I want her phone. Right before she said she was done talking, she got a text and smirked. Then she headed back toward the stables. Beau could have texted her and lured her out. Stone said he couldn't find Beau."

Stone pinched the bridge of his nose. "I'm not

sure Beau was having an affair with Talia. But we do need to know if the text came from him. Maybe he needed air and sat in the hay to take a breather, and he lost his wallet."

Emily gave him a *Get real* look, and he shrugged. "Just because Martin found her doesn't mean he didn't kill her. And having the chairman of the Texas Ethics Commission as his witness when he found her isn't too shabby. Royce Pemberton is known for his honesty and integrity—even if he was appointed by a governor who has neither of those traits."

"My question is if Martin Landers is trying to frame the governor because he knows about their affair, why not plant evidence that would lead back to the governor and incite an investigation from Emily? It's clear she can't be bought," Stone said.

"The affair itself is evidence," Bridge said. "You know about it. Or Martin realizes when you investigate—and you will—that you'll conclude this is yet another staged murder, which in itself connects to Paul. No need to plant outright evidence."

Stone's brother made a brilliant point. "We need to find out if Martin Landers was seen by any guests during the time Talia was in the stable for the second time."

"I'll ask around. Now that it's being ruled an

accident they're allowing guests to leave. Only family and close friends are here at the moment."

Emily frowned. Rhode was a close friend. He was there at every turn, knew the vics and he was loose-lipped. "Where is Beau?" She wanted to find him. Talk to him. "Have the police arrested him?"

"For what? Leaving his wallet in his own stable on accident? No. And he's not here. I haven't seen him."

"Well, he's never far from the other stooges. So where are they?" Stone asked.

"I don't know," Bridge said. "Rhode said he hadn't seen him in about an hour or so before they found the body, but Beau had been over the whole event and was talking about leaving."

"Look, we'll be back by later. After we find Beau." Stone ended the call and looked at Emily.

"I know where he might be." Sissy's voice drew their attention, though it was quiet. She stood in the doorway, her pooches flanking her. "I was getting water and overheard."

"Where's Mama?"

"Sleeping I think. I am capable of getting my own water. It's my shoulder that's been shot, not my feet."

"Where do you think he is?" Emily asked.

"There's a hole in the wall on the outskirts of Cedar Springs where he goes to play darts or pool. The patrons there aren't the kind to keep up with tabloids and the rich and famous. He likes to hang out there and not be recognized. Blows off steam." She shrugged. "Or he used to. But it's worth a shot. The place is called Lone Star."

"Thanks," Emily said.

Sissy nodded and shuffled to the kitchen.

"I'll go check it out," Stone said.

"I think not." Emily might feel like she'd been run over by a dump truck ten times, but she was not going to let Stone handle this alone. "Let me change and swallow down a few pain relievers, then I'm going too." She gave him a look that let him know it wasn't up for debate.

Twenty minutes later, they arrived at the cracker box called Lone Star. It was almost midnight and the gravel parking lot was scarce. Emily didn't notice a flashy car or truck that indicated the elite Beau Brighton was on the scene.

"That's his bike." Stone pointed to a modest Harley-Davidson parked next to others. "He's here."

Inside, the smell of smoke, sweat and beer filled the place. They pushed through the haze until they found Beau throwing darts with two other men. He was dressed like the rest of the patrons, in a pair of jeans and a flannel shirt, but he still stood out like a stallion in a pasture full of sheep in Emily's opinion.

He glanced up, then did a double take. "Y'all go on without me," he said to the two men, and he walked over. "What brings y'all here?" His eyes widened. "Is it Sissy?"

"No," Stone said firmly. "Have you not heard from anyone since you left the gala?"

"No. I left my phone in my room." He patted his front pockets and his back ones and scanned the dart area. "I must have forgotten my wallet too."

Emily scowled. What a great little thing to forget, along with his phone. He was clever. But she wasn't buying it. "Actually, you left that in the stable."

"I haven't been at the stables tonight."

TEN

Stone waited for Emily to pounce on Beau's lie.

"How well did you know Tiffany Williford—the judge's wife?" Emily asked instead. *Ah.* She was going to see how many more lies she could catch him in. She was a savvy investigator, which he respected. But why would Beau lie about being in the stables? Unless he was doing something that he felt warranted a lie.

"I only knew her through Judge."

Emily nodded and cocked her ear, frowning. The country Christmas music was deafening. "Can we step outside?" she asked.

"Sure."

Outside gave them less smoke, more privacy. "You knew Paisley, Lexi Bryant and Deidre Dillion too."

Beau's eyes narrowed. "Is that a question?"

"Where were you the nights of their deaths?"

Beau huffed. "What is going on? Why am I

starting to feel like a suspect to things that need no suspect?" He looked at Stone. "Do I need a lawyer, Stone? You know my father has an army of them."

Stone was well aware of the money and arsenal of attorneys within the Brighton family's reach. "Just indulge us, Beau. Where were you the nights of Tiffany's suicide, Deidre Dillion's accident, and Pai's and Lexi Bryant's deaths?"

Beau studied Stone as the reality of what was going on slowly dawned on him. "You don't think the accidents or suicides were either of those things. You think I would hurt Paisley? Or anyone?" Beau's jaw hardened when Stone remained silent. "The night Tiffany died, I was at home. Alone. Per usual. I'm sure an employee can vouch for me. As far as Deidre, I was in Palm Beach all weekend, and that night I went to Kiki Cruise's party. It was on her yacht."

"The movie star's daughter?" Stone asked.

"Yep."

"So, she can corroborate that?" Emily asked.

Beau's neck reddened. "I don't know. I didn't actually see her that night. I'm not sure who I saw or didn't see." He at least had the decency to shift his gaze to the floor. "I honestly have no idea where I was when Pai and Lexi died. It was a long time ago."

"One more question. You didn't go out to the

stable at all tonight? Or even earlier today?"
Stone asked.

"No."

Emily folded her arms over her chest. "I saw
you go out there, and your wallet was found in
a pile of hay just a few feet from Talia Landers's
body. So…why are you lying?"

Beau's wide-eyed gaze shifted from Emily to
Stone. "What? Talia's dead?"

"Talk to us, Beau. It's your best shot."

He hardened his jaw. "I see what's going on."

Yeah. Beau was caught with his hands in the
cookie jar.

"I am not saying one more word except *lawyer*. I'm done." He strode to his motorcycle and
spun gravel as he left.

"He'll have an attorney before first light."

"Fine." Emily rubbed her temples. "I don't
need him to get to the truth. I will find out why
he's lying about the stables and what was actually going on out there between him and Talia."

Stone put his arm around Emily. "Hey, let's
get back to the ranch. You need rest and so do I."

She didn't argue, which told him she was feeling worse than she let on. He led her to the car
and paused at the passenger door. Chills sent
hairs standing on his neck.

"I feel it too," Emily whispered. "As if we're
being watched."

"Yeah." He opened the door for her, and then he climbed in the driver's side. "Let's get home without a near-death experience if possible."

"Amen."

He drove warily and carefully home.

Inside, he filled a glass with water and swallowed down over-the-counter pain relievers. The last thing he needed was meds making him groggy or keeping him under. Emily followed suit.

"Good night," she murmured.

"You need anything else?" he asked, feeling the awkward tension and the ache to kiss her before she wandered to bed. But he refrained.

"No. I'm good. Tomorrow we'll look at Beau Brighton's connections to Paisley, Lexi, Deidre, Tiffany and even Talia Landers more closely. He's lying. He knows it and we know it. Now we have to find out why."

"Agreed. But try to sleep and not stay up all night wondering."

"I'll try."

"I'll set the security system. Get some sleep."

She nodded and left him alone in the kitchen. The ranch was dark except for the Christmas tree glowing and creating a cozy atmosphere. He hadn't even had a chance to shop yet. Maybe everyone would get a gift card this year. He could make a pass through the coffee shop drive through and—bada bing bada boom—he'd be done. Not creative. But his brain wasn't exactly firing on creative pistons at the moment.

After setting the security system with the app on his phone, he passed the living room, noticing Mama on the couch. "Mama," he said softly and nudged her shoulder, rousing her from sleep.

For a moment, she seemed disoriented, and then she smiled. "I was waiting up for you."

"Oh. Well, we're home and safe, and the security system has been set, so don't go outside."

She patted the place next to her and he sat down. Something was wrong. His stomach knotted.

"I was waiting to talk to you. I should have done it earlier today, yesterday even, but… I couldn't, and I was going to wait until after Christmas but so much is going on…"

"Mama, what is it?" Fear bolted through his veins, running cold. His mouth turned dry.

"I haven't been feeling well. As you may have suspected." Her smile wobbled.

He couldn't form a word. He nodded once.

"I went to the doctor about the fatigue. He ran some tests, and… I have leukemia, Stone."

Cancer.

The backs of his eyes burned and moisture flooded them, blurring his sight. "Are you sure?"

Mama took his clammy hand. "I'm sure."

His mother? Sick? *No. Not happening.* Spots formed in front of his eyes, but he held it together. He must. "Why did you go through the tests alone, Mama? I could have been there for you."

"Much like you didn't want to say anything until you knew for sure about Paisley's death, I too wanted to make sure it was real. No point being concerned if there was no need to be concerned." Her voice carried a slight tremor. "I'm not afraid. I'm nervous and at peace all at the same time."

He was not at peace. He was terrified. "What next?"

"Treatment." He listened, but his brain wasn't processing or retaining the treatment process or dates she outlined. He couldn't get past the C word. "I want to wait until after Christmas to tell the others."

But she'd told him. He had to bear it alone. He wasn't sure he could. They sat in silence for what felt like forever, and then he prayed for his mama and hugged her, never wanting to let go. This woman had bandaged his knees, disciplined him when he'd misbehaved, baked him brownies over cake on his birthdays and guided him through his first heartbreak over a girl. She was the glue that stuck this family together— not him. Not really. Though he felt it most of the time. A lump grew in his throat, tight and painful. He couldn't swallow.

Finally, she released him. "I'm tired."

He was exhausted. Drained. "Yeah, get rest. You need it."

Mama stood and folded the blanket, then draped it over the couch. He walked her to her bedroom and lightly kissed her cheek. "Call me if you need anything."

"I will." She patted his scruffy face and slipped into her bedroom.

How was he supposed to deal with this? Fix this? Make it better? His heart beat fast and his head swam. Not good for the high blood pressure. He trudged down the hall and paused at Emily's door. He raised his hand to knock. To confide. This was too big. Too much. But she had enough on her plate and needed sleep. Instead he entered his dark room. Stone didn't bother turning on the lamp light. He collapsed on his bed and soaked his pillows in tears.

Sleep had come easier than Emily expected. This morning, she was the first one up, so she decided to make breakfast for the family. She wasn't the greatest chef, but she knew how to make pancakes. It was the least she could do for all their hospitality. She pilfered through the kitchen and found the ingredients, ignoring her sore body and the dull thump behind her eyes. Stitches were tender. But she was alive, and she would find out who was behind these staged deaths.

It very well may kill her, but she wouldn't stop. She couldn't.

Her phone beeped. Another text from Dottie. Maybe it was time to call her half sister. To hear her side. But she couldn't do it. Instead, she texted back.

I'm sorry I haven't taken your calls or answered your texts. I just need some time. Dad was my whole world, and now I'm not sure what to think or believe. Please give me time.

A text reply came immediately.

I understand. We feel the same way. Betrayed and confused. I'll give you space. When you're ready, please know I want to talk to you, meet you. But I won't call or text again. Merry Christmas.

Maybe now was the time to talk to Mom about reaching out to Dottie. Since the case wasn't wrapped up, Emily was sticking around, and maybe Mom would want to go to the reimagined zoo that was now a park with hiking trails and a venue for other events. She'd lead with that.

Mom answered on the second ring, and they made small talk.

Emily led with the zoo event, but Mom was going to church Christmas Eve. "I really wish you'd come."

"I might be able to get a chance. We'll see. Um… Mom. Dad's other daughter has been texting. I need time, but I was thinking maybe I should talk to her."

Mom sighed, and too many beats went with silence. Finally, she spoke. "I can't really blame the other family, Emily. As much as I would like to continue to do so. Blame rests squarely on your father's shoulders. So if you decide to call her, then I won't stop you."

"You won't feel betrayed? I thought you said we were in it alone, and they could fend for themselves."

She laughed, but there was little humor in it. "I did. But I've had time to think, process and pray. We were betrayed. But not by them. You should call her when you feel ready."

As Emily mixed up pancake batter, they talked through the tough situation. It looked like Mom had dealt with the initial shock and pain. Like Emily. Still, she wasn't quite ready to talk with Dottie.

"I love you," she said.

"I love you too, honey. Be safe and try to come to church Christmas Eve."

She would. After ending the call, turning on a

Christmas playlist from her phone and whipping up a platter of pancakes, she saw Stone enter the kitchen looking like death. His scruff was now a day-old beard, his hair disheveled and his eyes bloodshot.

"Did you not sleep?" Emily asked.

"No," he said through a rasp and took in the spread. "You cooked?"

"And I didn't burn a thing."

He grinned. "Why did you cook?"

"As a thank-you and because I wanted to. You hungry?"

His face said, *Not really*, but he nodded. "Yeah."

"Liar liar pants on fire." She came around the island. "What zapped your appetite?"

Stone looked around and pawed his face. "My mom told me last night she has leukemia. She doesn't want anyone else to know until after the holidays. She's put off treatment until then."

Emily's heart stammered. "Oh, Stone." She encircled him, wrapping her arms tightly around his waist, leaning into his chest. His strong arms came around her for comfort, and he laid his chin gently on the top of her head.

"I don't know what to do. I can't fix this one, Em."

"No. But you can pray and be there for her." She rubbed his back, hoping he felt her comfort. She leaned her head back. "We'll get through it."

"We?" he murmured and slid a stray hair from her face, tucking it behind her ear.

"Yeah. We're friends, right? And friends are there for one another." She didn't deny they were more than colleagues, that she wanted him as a friend. A good friend.

"Absolutely. I heard you on the phone with your mom. She okay?"

"Yeah." She told him what they discussed.

"You going to call Dottie?"

"I am. I think I want to. I want to see her. Being around your family has reminded me how much I did want siblings. But now isn't the time. Not with all the danger. Once this case wraps up, I'm going to reach out."

"I can go with you. You know, together. That's what friends are for, right?"

She grinned, liking that idea a lot. "Absolutely."

"Am I interrupting?" Sissy asked.

They broke apart and Emily's cheeks heated. "No. I made breakfast. How do you feel today?"

"Sore but better." She eyed the platter on the table. "I love pancakes."

"Have at 'em." Emily's news app alerted her, and she swiped up. A tabloid headline popped up, and dread dug a cold pit in Emily's stomach.

"What's wrong?" Stone asked.

She held up the news article with a big fat picture of Beau Brighton with each of the victims, but one stood out. He and Deidre Dillion on a yacht in the Bahamas one week before she died and another photo the day of her death at his place when he said he was in Palm Beach that weekend. "And the lies keep on coming."

Stone skimmed the article. "Beau Brighton: Texas Royalty, Naughty or Nice?"

The article went on to note that sources said a Texas Ranger was investigating the deaths of at least four women: Paisley Spencer, Lexi Bryant, Deidre Dillion and Tiffany Williford. That their suicides and accidents might be murder and that Texas royalty bad boy Beau Brighton can be connected to each woman.

They must really want to get slapped with a lawsuit.

"How did this all get leaked? By whom?" Emily asked, seething.

"I don't know. Not Beau," Sissy said. "That makes no sense."

"I want to talk to the journalist who wrote this piece," Emily said.

Stone nodded. "What's her name?"

She skimmed the post. "Rachel Dillingham. With the *Texas Scoop*, 'where everything's bigger, including the stories.' What a ridiculous tagline." This reporter had no idea what she'd just done. "This might get her killed, Stone. We need to move fast, if for no other reason than to warn her."

She hurried and dressed for the day and met Stone in the foyer. As they made their way to her car, she noticed a manila envelope on her windshield.

"You see what I see?"

"Yep, already pulling up security footage on my phone."

Emily rushed to her car and opened her trunk. She rummaged through her kit and found a pair of gloves and an evidence bag. She brought Stone a pair of gloves as well, and then she carefully took the envelope. Inside was a note.

STOP NOW OR PEOPLE YOU LOVE ARE GOING TO DIE.

Breath left her lungs as she handed it to Stone. "There's something else in here." She pulled a paper out of the envelope and her knees buckled. Stone reached out to steady her.

It was a black-and-white photo of her mom sitting in her living room reading. She hadn't a single clue that someone had reached inside her home with a telephoto lens and captured her on film. "Stone, my mom..."

"We'll get her somewhere safe. ASAP. Before

we even talk to Rachel Dillingham. Bridge has experience with this. He can help."

"I can't trust anyone. I need to get her somewhere myself." *But where?* Emily had nowhere to take her. No one to help. "She can't come here. We've already been in danger. I need to get her out of town or something."

"You can trust me, Emily." The hurt in his voice reached her ears; she hated that she'd hurt him. But somehow she couldn't make her head get in the same game as her heart.

She studied the photo again. *Mom.* They were going to kill her if she didn't back down.

But could she?

Could Emily ignore the justice of four maybe five women to save her mom?

ELEVEN

Emily rubbed her temples, which didn't help her headache, and her chest felt as if it were buried beneath a ton of concrete. She and Stone had left her mom's place about an hour ago after revealing that she might be in danger. And after further discussion, they'd decided bringing Mom to the ranch was the safest avenue after all. They had no access to a safe house, and someone kept a few steps ahead of them, so sending her off somewhere secluded might be worse than bringing her to the Spencer Ranch. At least there was security and a number of people with a law enforcement background.

Mom had protested, but after Emily stressed just how serious it was, she agreed. She'd packed a suitcase and they'd brought her to the ranch. She would bunk with Emily.

Now they walked up the street to the *Texas Scoop* offices located in downtown Austin, where they could talk to tabloid writer Rachel

Dillingham. Emily scoured her surroundings. She didn't wonder if they were being watched; she knew they were. Now with this article, it would bring out the media in droves. Everything she was hoping to avoid.

But the finger hadn't been pointed at the governor. It had been pointed at Beau. He had lied and might be involved, but if not, he was being set up to take the heat off Paul Henderson.

Was Rachel Dillingham in on it?

They approached the tall white office building. The glass doors were so clean Emily could see her reflection as well as in a mirror. She'd left her hair down. Her scalp was too tender to pull it up. And she was in dressier jeans and a cream sweater. She actually missed her uniform. But she was still on vacation, even though it sure didn't feel like one.

"Bridge called while you were getting your mom settled. He'd like to take a crack at the ME who signed off on the accidents and suicides now that the tabloid has leaked the news. Other reporters will be wondering about the rulings. The ME might be willing to talk if he thinks his job is on the line."

"It's worth a shot. At this point, there's no hiding from anyone. No reason to be discreet other than using the governor's name. We still need to tread lightly there." She faced him. "What about Rhode? What's he doing?" Didn't seem like much. He rarely weighed in on discussions, but he was there to hear all the details and updates. Was he relaying it all back to Beau or Martin or even the governor?

"I haven't heard from him today. But Bridge says they'll keep watch over the ranch. They can work from their phones and laptops. One will be there at all times as long as our moms are there."

She did appreciate that. While she didn't really trust Rhode to do his job, she also didn't think he'd put his own mother in harm's way. "Thank you," she said. "He going to keep tabs on the Cedar Springs homicide detective who is lead on Tiffany's case?"

"Yeah. It's a Detective Neil Lang. Seems like a straight arrow, but since Tiffany's photos are 'misplaced'—" he made air quotes with his fingers "—who knows. Rhode worked with him and says he finds it hard to believe he was on the take, but he'll dig."

Another person Rhode was close to. A homicide detective where Rhode used to work. She kept her mouth closed though. Instead, she said, "Little convenient they lost or misplaced those crime scene photos that no doubt would show proof Tiffany was murdered. Now that it's out, I'm going to see if I can formally request the autopsy photos of all the women. They can't all be misplaced."

"I guess we'll see."

They entered the building, which was decked for Christmas with garlands and red bows. It smelled of cinnamon and vanilla, not lies and slander. "I hate these sleazy tabloids, but today it'll work in my favor. I hope."

They climbed the stairs to the second floor, where the *Texas Scoop* offices were located, and approached the reception desk.

Emily showed her Texas Ranger badge. "Texas Ranger Emily O'Connell to see Rachel Dillingham, please. I don't have an appointment, but tell her it's in regard to Beau Brighton."

The wide-eyed young woman rushed to get Rachel Dillingham on the line, then conveyed the message. "She'll see you."

She thought she would.

Emily and Stone followed the receptionist to a private corner cubicle. Miss Dillingham was already standing. The size of a middle schooler, with dark hooded eyes and a hungry but perfect smile, Rachel held out her hand as introductions were made then escorted them to the conference room for privacy and surprisingly good coffee.

Emily spoke first. She would control this narrative. "Can you tell us where the photos of Beau Brighton with the women came from?"

"A fake email account, I'd venture to guess. We get that often. Our people did verify the photos were real—no Photoshop, no fake date stamps. Can I ask why? There's been some buzz that you're looking into Tiffany Williford's murder, and it's put you in the line of fire and you're taking up residence for now at Mr. Spencer's ranch. Is that true?"

This lady was smooth and intelligent. If she wasn't writing for a garbage magazine, Emily might like her. But Emily wasn't the one being interviewed. "Any message in the email besides what it said in the article?"

Rachel studied Emily a few seconds. "Yes." She handed them a paper.

Emily read it.

Beau Brighton isn't what he seems. He connects to four women who died, but Texas Ranger Emily O'Connell is quietly investigating these deaths. Why would she do that unless the suicides and accidents were actual murders? And why Beau Brighton? He's not a state employee, but has the investigation led to him?

"I didn't include the other comments. Just enough for readers to be enticed," Rachel said.

"Yes. By all means let's entice readers." Emily

held back an eye roll. Coming right off the heels of questioning Beau, the email was odd. She and Stone had felt watched at the bar last night. Or maybe Beau told the wrong person he'd been questioned and felt like a suspect. Someone who saw his confidence as an opportunity to sell him out or reveal he was the killer without revealing their own identity. They needed to talk to Beau again. "Anything else you've heard?"

Rachel grinned, her glossy red lipstick not even bleeding. "Heard? No. Suspect? Yes. That someone wants you onto Beau because he killed those women, or they want you on him and off of them. Brighton's a real character. I've done several pieces on him. Texas loves him. I'm not a fan though. Were you initially investigating him or Tiffany Williford? I assume the woman entering the judge's house the day she died is you, but not in your uniform to be discreet. Which means you initially thought it was the judge."

This woman was good and had done her homework.

"You know I can't comment on an ongoing case."

Rachel crossed her legs and batted her glance between Stone and Emily. "I'll strike a deal with you. If I can get you the IP address of the computer that sent the email, when this case breaks, you give me the exclusive. *Not* for the tabloid."

She leaned forward. "I was an investigative journalist with a real news station—once." She sighed. "This isn't my dream. It pays the bills. I'll write it freelance."

"Maybe get back in the game of reputable news."

Rachel hooted. "It's been awhile since the news has been labeled reputable."

Emily agreed. "Okay. But listen to me carefully. Don't go digging on your own. Just see if you can trace the address the email came from. Say nothing to anyone. I don't care if you think you can trust them. Don't. Okay?"

Rachel's dark eyes widened and Emily knew she got the hint. This was big. Real big and real scary, and it could get her killed. "Understood, Ranger." They traded business cards.

Then Rachel smiled at Stone, who had remained unusually quiet. "I admire you for stepping out of the Texas Rangers to build an aftermath recovery business. I admire that a lot."

Her sparkling eyes said she admired more than that, and Emily felt a pinch of green in her gut.

"Thank you," Stone said.

"I'd love to do a piece on you sometime when this investigation is over." She blinked, her long lashes accenting her exotic eyes. She had pale, smooth skin—no freckles. Another pinch of jealousy.

But the audacity! Emily was standing right here! Still, she had to admit Rachel was subtle. Smooth.

Stone smirked. "I don't really do interviews, Miss Dillingham. Good day."

"Good day," she said and watched them walk away.

"Well, she was into you," Emily said as soon as they were in the hallway.

"Well, I'm not into her." He opened the door for Emily. "Not my type."

"No?" she asked as they stepped into the cool December air. Not cold. Not exactly warm either today. "What's your type?"

"Oh, the feisty kind who can burn dinner but pull off pancakes and never get her timing right for relationships. She probably turns down dinner invitations for tacos and guac too, but I'm just spitballing." He shoved his hands in his pockets, shrugged and winked, then strode a little ahead of her.

She was glad too, because her stomach dropped, and her face felt like flames of fire had exploded in them. He was right about one thing for sure. Her timing was so off. But so was his.

"I want to talk with Beau again," she said evading further flirting or having to address what wasn't going to be between them.

"I do too. It's no coincidence that the photos were leaked late last night after Talia Landers was murdered and Beau questioned." He paused. "That was another thing Bridge said. Talia's death was ruled an accident. Horse kicked her. Someone could have bashed her head in and said it was a horse, but forensics should be able to conclude the truth. Bridge texted me while we were in the meeting with the reporter. He wants to call a friend in the FBI to look into that. With your permission."

Emily got inside the car. "I don't know. Is the agent from a Texas field office?"

"No. Actually, Tennessee. A corruption task force."

Her hands were tied. She may not have much trust, but she was at a point where she couldn't afford not to. "Okay. Keep it on the QT though."

"I promise. You can trust me. You can trust us."

"I'm counting on it, Stone. Please don't let me down."

"I won't." He touched her cheek. "Now what?"

"Now we talk to Beau. After the photos leaking, he may want to say more than 'lawyer.'"

Twenty minutes into the ride to Brighton Ranch, Emily's phone rang. "It's Rachel Dillingham." She answered and placed the call on speaker.

"Hi, Miss Dillingham. Didn't expect to hear from you this fast."

"Well, not everyone is adept in hiding. The photos of Beau Brighton were sent from a dummy account, which we already knew, but we traced it and got the IP address. And it's very interesting. I really do want the exclusive."

"You have my word, Miss Dillingham. Now, who sent that email?"

"Paul Henderson Junior."

The governor's son.

"PJ? Why would he send photos of Beau with the victims?" Stone asked after Emily ended the call. "He and Beau are best friends."

Emily frowned. "He either thinks Beau did it and didn't want to get too involved, or he knows his dad is in trouble, so he sent the email to frame Beau."

"Or one last option. Someone sent it from PJ's IP address."

"I guess the best we can do is ask him ourselves. Where would he be?"

"Rhode would probably know or be able to find out." He called his brother, and he answered on the fourth ring.

"What's up?" Rhode asked.

"I need you to find out or tell me, if you know, where PJ is right now."

"Why?" Rhode asked, wary.

"Because I need to know." He glanced at

Emily, who was eyeing him with a *tread lightly* look. She'd made nice with Rhode until the gala, then it had gone to pot, and neither had worked to make it right yet. She had zero faith in him, and Stone had to admit his brother was acting squirrely. But these were his best friends.

"He'd mentioned playing racquetball at the Austin Country Club. I'll text him and see. Just hold on. This whole thing is absurd. Beau. Now PJ. I think I'd know if one of my friends was a killer. I'm a homicide detective—" he paused "—was. I mean, who next? Trystan? Me? I can connect to all the victims too."

"Then give us your alibis," Emily said coolly.

Stone bristled and the line grew quiet.

"You can have mine when you also ask for Stone's and Bridge's. They also knew the victims. Maybe not well, but, hey, no one seems to care." He huffed. "PJ's there now. Court six." He ended the call without a goodbye.

"Let's go talk to PJ then we can circle back to Beau."

"Agreed."

Stone plugged in the country club address to his phone, and the automated GPS voice began navigating them.

"Rhode's sensitive," Stone said. "Been trying to build back his reputation, and this case is needling him."

Jessica R. Patch 213

"You mean I'm needling him. Trust has to be earned. And even then, it's a thin line. I did some digging. I know he was a good homicide detective. Very astute."

"He was. He still is—astute. He's a great PI, and he's building up his practice. He's afraid this will cause him to take a hit." Stone sighed. "I worry about him."

"Because he's an alcoholic?"

Stone nodded. "I don't want all this pressure to send him into a spiral."

Emily merged into traffic and concentrated on the congestion. Stone let her focus. She listened as the GPS gave instruction, and soon they turned into the parking lot of the country club.

"I'll try to be nicer to Rhode. I don't want that either," she said.

"Thank you."

They stepped out of the vehicle. The clouds were gray and heavy. Rain was coming. No snow. Rarely ever did it snow for Christmas in Texas, but the two times in his entire life it did, it was insanely wonderful.

Inside the club, they asked for directions to court six and were escorted there. Badge or not, they weren't members. And nonmembers couldn't be flitting around the establishment, which smelled of fresh linens, cigar smoke and money.

Thwack! Thwack! Thwack!

The sounds of rubber balls being smacked against walls echoed as they approached the last court on the right. PJ was dressed in white shorts and a white shirt with a white towel hanging around his sweaty neck. His sandy brown hair hung limp around his forehead.

"Stone! You old goat, you up for a round? What brings you here?" PJ shook his hand and nodded at Emily. "Nice to see you again." He didn't seem to put together the fact that they were here in a professional capacity—or he didn't care. "Is this about Talia?"

Guess he didn't care.

His dark blue eyes softened. "That was... I don't even know. Martin is on leave right now. Instead of finalizing his Christmas plans to the islands, he's planning a funeral. Life isn't fair, is it?"

"No. It's not."

"No," he echoed. "I can't tell you much about Talia other than she had a big hand in helping fund Janice's nonprofit. She and Tiffany Williford. Another tragic situation."

"True." Stone let him ramble. See where he'd go, if he'd spill any information they didn't already have. Emily seemed to be thinking the same thing, as she kept quiet too.

He wiped the sweat from his brow with his towel and looked to Stone then to Emily. "That's all I really know about Talia. Other than we all hung out as kids. She was from Dallas though. Her dad's a judge."

Talia couldn't be connected by family to a fraternity brother, or directly, according to Bridge's fast work. She was the odd woman out there. Who knows? Maybe she had been kicked by a horse.

"Did you know Tiffany before she married Judge Williford?" Emily asked. "Did Beau Brighton know her prior to her marriage to the judge?"

PJ slung his towel back over his shoulder, the scent of musk and sweat reaching Stone's nostrils. "I think she came from Florida, but we all knew her before she married Judge. Women like Tiffany like to infiltrate the wealthy political circle, then go on the hunt for who's eligible. They really don't care who it is, or how old or young. The real question is do they have money. And in these circles—yes, we do."

Stone arched an eyebrow. "So you think Tiffany was a gold digger? What about Deidre?"

"Deidre?" he asked and cleared this throat, looking away. "She had her own money. What's she got to do with anything?"

"How about you tell us?" Stone asked. "PJ, if you know something about Beau, you have to tell us more. You've already told us something." He folded his arms over his chest, waiting. Folks didn't like silence. Silence made people uncomfortable. So he let PJ be uncomfortable.

PJ's face crumpled, and he pawed it as if trying to right it. "You know I leaked the photos."

"I do." He waited. Emily waited. He was a little shocked she wasn't interrupting, but while her eyes were intense, she was stoic.

PJ groaned. "I love Beau. He's one of my best friends. You know this. We're the Rat Pack."

Three Stooges, but he let it go.

"He told me you questioned him last night about his alibis, not just for Tiffany but Deidre, Paisley and even Lexi. I was like, 'That's insane,' but I also knew he'd been in the stable with Talia last night. I saw him go out there, and I saw her go out there too."

"How did you see them? Where were you?" Emily now spoke up.

"I was outside. I needed a breather. I'm not saying I don't like my dad's money or power. I'd be stupid to say I don't. But I also have a lot of pressure on me to pursue the same political career, which I don't want. And it's no real secret I don't exactly get along with my father. But if I don't do things his way, I get cut off."

Boo-hoo. So he might have to do something productive with his life and earn a living. Might make a man out of him. He was almost thirty-five years old, and Stone wasn't sure he'd ever held down a job that his father hadn't handed to him, and even then, it never lasted. He lived off his trust fund, and it was enough to buy a fleet of yachts and sail the world ten times over.

"Why did you send the photos?"

"Because I loved Deidre. I really did. Beau— he knows he's all that, and he never cares about anyone else. She got swept up in his charm, and things cooled between us. I knew it wouldn't last with Beau, because you know him as well as I do. Beau sees a shiny toy. Beau chases the shiny toy. Beau gets the shiny toy and Beau throws the shiny toy away when he's bored. Which doesn't take long."

Stone most certainly knew that about Beau. To Beau, women were a challenge. Once they were conquered, he moved on to the next. He brought the topic back to PJ. "So you wanted revenge."

"No." He shook his head. "No way. If Beau did something to Deidre—to any of those women— I want justice. Just so you know, Rachel Dillingham isn't some skank tabloid reporter. She's from Washington. An investigative journalist and a good one. I purposely sent it to her. Yeah, she posted it. But she'll sniff out a story, a real one. That's what I want."

"But if he's innocent, you might ruin his reputation," Stone said.

PJ laughed. "He doesn't have a stellar reputation, Stone, though Texas still loves him because he oozes charm. That's why I did it anonymously.

If he's innocent, he's none the wiser that I was skeptical. That I was curious."

"Why not just come to me? Privately."

Snorting, PJ waved his hand. "Beau is Rhode's ride or die. I couldn't trust you not saying something."

Emily shifted her weight to her other foot and inhaled. Great, PJ was confirming her false idea that Rhode and even Stone couldn't be trusted.

"You know me better than that," Stone rebuked.

"I also know blood is thicker than water. Why do you think I never say anything publicly about my dad and all his affairs—including the one with Talia Landers? Yeah, I know. Everyone knows."

"Your mom know?"

"My mom lives in blissful ignorance—or denial. Either way, deep down she knows." PJ's hardened jaw over his dad's dalliances could be motive to frame him, but why send a photo of Beau and toss him under the bus if he was getting back at his own father? That didn't make sense unless Stone was missing a piece of the puzzle.

"What do you think Beau was doing in the stable with Talia? Could she have been messing around with your dad and Beau?" Stone asked.

PJ's brow knit. "I don't think so. Beau never mentioned it, and he typically enjoys flaunting his victories. I really can't say why he was in there, but I know that he was. I'm not saying it's not possible. It might have been a real fun challenge to have an affair with the same woman as the governor. And he's never made it secret that he didn't like Martin. But I always thought it was because Martin always wanted Sissy. He settled for Talia."

Stone had his suspicions that Martin had always had a thing for Sissy. But Sissy, in the early days, only had eyes for Beau. Until that went sideways and she later ended up falling for Todd and marrying him.

The plot was thickening for sure. "Do you think Beau killed these women?" He needed to ask outright.

"I don't know." PJ pinched the bridge of his nose. "He told me he was questioned and that he lied about his alibi. I just wanted someone to know he was lying. Even to me. He was with Deidre the day she died. People I'm around all the time hide who they really are, Stone. You know this. Would you have ever thought Rhode would do what he did?"

Emily bristled again and Stone inwardly cringed. "No. But he wasn't pretending to be someone he wasn't. He had mitigating circumstances."

"Mitigating circumstances? That's what you're

calling being drunk and losing key evidence in a homicide case?" PJ asked and his eyes narrowed. "Well, that wouldn't have held up in a court of law if it had made it that far. And my dad saw that it didn't."

Was that a low-key threat to steer clear of his dad or just a fact? When had this become about Rhode anyway?

PJ looked at Emily. "I wish I had more answers. And I probably should have brought the photos to you. I know who you are, what unit you work in, and I also know that you just lost your director. I'm thinking someone doesn't want you to know what's really going on."

"Does Beau have that kind of pull?" Emily asked.

"When you have more money than a McDuck, yeah. Yeah, I'd say you do."

"What about your dad?" She cocked her head.

"My dad doesn't need to kill women to keep them quiet." He checked his watch.

"One more question," Emily said. "Are you implying that your dad had affairs with Tiffany Williford, Deidre Dillion, Lexi Bryant and Paisley Spencer?"

Stone's gut knotted something fierce. He didn't want to believe it. Couldn't.

PJ batted his glance between them, then landed his sight on Stone. "If Paisley wasn't included, I'd say maybe. It's possible. But not her, Stone. Not Pai."

Relaxing, Stone nodded. He needed to hear that, but he still had a case to work.

"If you think of anything else, please contact me," Emily said as she handed PJ her card. "Thank you for your time."

Once out of earshot, Emily said, "We need to have a briefing. With everyone. Run these ideas by both Bridge and Rhode," she said through a tight voice. "We're no closer to finding out the truth, and now my mom has been threatened."

"We'll catch a break. And we'll keep her safe."

But deep in his bones, he knew time for all of them was running out.

"Stone!" Stone turned, and Judge Williford stood at the entrance to the club. "I thought that was you. Can I talk to you for a few moments?"

Emily waved him off. "Go. Maybe he'll give you some information on Tiffany. I'll go to the car and make a phone call."

"Okay. Be right back."

"What did I say about that?"

He smirked at their previous talk about horror movies. "I *will* be back."

Emily chuckled. "Is this our bit?"

"I like it. I like that we have a bit. Also, lock the doors. I'd feel better."

But not much.

TWELVE

Emily wanted to check in on her mom. She headed for the car and pulled out her phone. But before she clicked on her name, a wave of awareness stopped her dead in her tracks.

She reached for her gun, for reassurance, as a masked man sprung from behind the car next to hers and lunged at her, knocking her down and nearly causing her to drop her weapon.

They wrestled for the piece, and in the scuffle, it slid across the pavement out of reach. Her heart thudded against her ribs, and adrenaline raced through her blood as her fight-or-flight reflex kicked in. She rammed her hand up toward his masked nose, but he ducked before she could make solid contact to break it.

His gloved hands wrapped around her neck and began squeezing. She couldn't go for his eyes; they were covered behind dark lenses underneath his mask. Her lungs flamed, and white light dotted her vision. She rammed him with her knee, and he released his hold.

She screamed. "Fire! Fire!"

The attacker reared back and brought his fist down, but she rolled her head to the side, and he pounded pavement and howled, giving her time to maneuver out from under him and scramble for the gun.

She got to it just as he did. He slammed her hand down on the asphalt, sending a jarring sensation through her entire arm and into her head, but she held on to the gun.

"Emily!"

Stone.

The attacker snapped to attention, slammed her hand down again, this time forcing her to release the weapon, then he sprang up and kicked her in the ribs. She sucked in and curled into a ball at the rush of pain.

Sprinting, the man darted between cars as Stone pursued. She lost her breath. Needed a minute. She didn't think he cracked her ribs, but they would be bruised for a long time. She couldn't help Stone. Couldn't even get to her feet. Finally, she gripped the side of the car and used it to help her stand and regain her balance.

Stone returned. "You're hurt," he said.

"Ribs," she rasped. "Not at all pleasant." She tried for a good-hearted grin, but it fell flat.

"You need a doctor."

"No. I'm over them. I'm guessing you lost him?" She allowed him to help her to the car. "You drive," she muttered and handed him her purse, no energy to even dig out her keys.

After helping her into the passenger seat, Stone jumped inside. "I lost him." He pounded the steering wheel. "And I got nothing from Williford. He saw the article today. He's furious. I told him the photos of his wife were missing, and that only fueled his fire. He wanted information. I told him I'm not working a case. But our family history goes back, so he assumed he'd get information based on our personal friendship."

"Did he get it?" she asked.

He tsked and shook his head. "You're never going to trust me, are you? No. No, he did not get any information. I don't work that way."

Laying her head back, she didn't want to get into it again. And she flat out had no energy to apologize. But she would. Again. *Lord, help me get a handle on this. I don't want to be this way, and yet I am. Ugh.*

They rode in silence except for the phone calls Stone made to Bridge and Rhode, letting them know to be ready for a briefing when they arrived at the ranch.

Once there, she eased down on the couch, and Stone brought her an ice pack but said nothing.

Rhode and Bridge took a seat, and Sissy sat next to her, the dogs loving on her. Emily could get with that. She'd like a little cavalier for herself. One day maybe. After everyone asked about her, she relayed the new information.

"I've had time to think about it." Especially since she and Stone hadn't talked on the ride home. "I don't trust PJ." She held up her hand. "I know. I don't trust anyone, but I work for the Public Integrity Unit. I see what greed and corruption does. And I have some personal experience. But hear me out. PJ makes no bones about his dislike of his father or his ways. What if he did it hoping we'd blame his father? Which we have. But the investigation takes another turn. Now we're interviewing others, including the victims' friends. So why not throw Beau under the bus? He's innocent. We'll find out he's innocent, and we'll point fingers back at the governor again. Never assume PJ was setting up dear old dad. After all, he was willing to shed truth on Beau, who is his best friend."

"It's not an implausible theory," Stone said.

Emily shifted on the couch. "If Beau is innocent, then that photo with Deidre is just a photo. It proves he lied about being with her. Not killing her. We have no evidence or motive. PJ is smart. He went to law school. He knows at the end of the day, Beau isn't going to trial or prison, because he didn't do it."

"Unless he did," Stone added.

"He didn't," Rhode interjected. "And neither did PJ. This is nuts."

Emily shot him a daggered look, and he had the decency to shut up. "I want to look good and hard at Paul Henderson Junior. If the photos came from PJ's phone, then he took the photo of Beau with Deidre, which means he was with her the night she died too. He's unaccounted for during the time Talia died. And quite frankly, he had time to change and attack me at the country club while you were talking with the judge."

Stone heaved a breath. "She's right. I don't want to believe it, but last time I ignored my gut, I let Paisley's death go down as a suicide and didn't look for justice. We have to at least consider our friend—Rhode, your friend—might be involved. Might be guilty. Women are continuing to die."

Rhode's jaw pulsed. "Fine. But when my friends aren't found guilty, I expect a big fat steak dinner."

Stone snorted. "Bridge, did you make contact with the FBI agent to work the Cedar Springs law enforcement or the ME?"

"I did. He's flying out to Texas tonight. The

ME has been conveniently out of the office and unable to take my calls."

Stone huffed. "Okay. Let's rest. We need it." His accusing gaze landed on her.

Emily didn't argue. She was flat out spent.

Emily's night had been ripe with weird dreams. Her ribs were sore this morning but at least she could breathe without wanting to die.

She was able to pull her hair in a loose knot on her back of her neck, and she'd slipped into a sweater and jeans and cowboy boots. Her worn favorite ones. Never knew who she might have to kick today. A killer. Stone. Possibly his brother. Might as well wear the weapon.

The kitchen was quiet when she went to pour herself a cup of coffee. She sat down and opened up her phone and saw an email from the reporter at the *Texas Scoop*.

Thought you should know. I dug. Sorry. I'm a digger. I didn't come up with much, but PJ Henderson left the country on a private plane before dawn this morning. And you'll be thrilled to know (that is sarcasm btw) he's gone to Morocco, which as you know has no extradition laws. Imagine that. He's either afraid for his life or he's guilty of something. The weather is much better in the Caymans right now. Just sayin'.

One last note. Everything I read on Stone Spencer is honorable, but you should know I found out that the governor gave a substantial amount of money to his father about a decade or so ago and then six months before he died. It appears the ranch was in dire straits, and the money kept them in the home and afloat. And we all know nothing is truly free.
—Rachel Dillingham

Emily set her coffee cup on the table, dazed and furious and confused. If PJ was setting up his dad and throwing the law off him by submitting the anonymous photos, why leave the country? Unless he got scared they would peel back the stinking onion and find the truth. Now, if they did, he would be in a country where they could do nothing about it, and with his money, he could die there of a nice old age.

She pounded the table with her fist as Stone made his entrance.

"Good morning?" His question was far from amusing.

No one even knew they wanted to investigate PJ except those in the living room last night. Stone. Bridge. Sissy. And Rhode. It's the only way PJ could have known. He'd been tipped off by a Spencer!

"No, it is not." She couldn't control the fury

in her tone. She'd gone against her instincts, believed and trusted, and now PJ Henderson was gone. Poof! "I trusted you," she said.

"Yeah. And?"

She spewed Rachel Dillingham's email about PJ, holding back, for now, the news about the money given to his family. It's possible Stone didn't know, but he was the new Spencer patriarch, so surely he did. "No one but this household knew we even suspected PJ. Not even PJ—it was going in his favor actually, if he's the killer. We asked about Beau and his father. He might have been framing both of them. But now we'll never know, and if we do discover it's him, he's gone. Gone! I trusted you, Stone. Was it you? Did you tip him off?"

Stone's jaw hardened and his eyes narrowed. "I have been nothing but helpful, and I've bent over backward to make you see I'm on your side. I've put my life in jeopardy, Emily. For *you*!" His soft-edged voice rose. "You. Why would I do that? Why would a killer shoot me or try to drown me if I was on his side? You're not making any rational sense." He stepped closer. "I have been trustworthy, and I don't know what else I can do to prove it but die for you. And even then, I don't think it would be enough, Emily!"

Her entire body shook. "So what? You're saying you put yourself on the line to earn my trust?

And because of that, I owe you my life too? I owe you that blind trust?" *Unbelievable*. "Rachel was right. Nothing is for free. Maybe you've been helping out the good old governor because he helped out your good old dad. Saved this ranch and saved your family from bankruptcy not once but twice!"

Stone took a visible step backward. No words. He had no words because he was guilty. He felt he owed the governor a tip. To return the favor. That's all she ever saw in this job. Greed. Scratching backs. Morality destroyed, and corruption infiltrated lives of people who went in with honorable notions to serve the state of Texas. But you didn't jump in the deep end with a bunch of sharks without learning how to eat like one.

He hadn't denied the money handoff or the tip-off, she realized. Just like the rest of the slime. Evade. Dance. Never admit. Tears sprung to her eyes. "I let myself be vulnerable with you. I... kissed you! You think I do that lightly? I don't." Everything she felt bubbled to the surface, and she couldn't control it if she wanted to. "I thought I might be falling in love with you. And I don't want to, Stone! I don't *want* to love you. I don't even want to *care* about you. I can't. Even if you didn't tip off PJ, you didn't tell me the whole truth about your connections with the governor."

She threw up her hands. "I can't have secrets. I won't. I'm just… I'm done."

She blew past him, leaving him with his mouth hanging open.

As she stormed into the living room, she heard him holler, "We never even got started! And since when are you a quitter, O'Connell?"

Outside, she pressed the heels of her hands to her eyes. She wasn't a quitter. But Dad's lies had colored everything, and not in a rosy kind of way. What had she done? Said? Bringing love into it? This was professional trust he'd crossed or allowed to be crossed. He was blinded by his brother. Or by family connections. Maybe he didn't think this one tip would matter. Who knows?

She collapsed on the porch steps and laid her head on her knees. Her body was like a shaken-up Coke bottle, but she refused to blow and bawl and squall. One hissy fit was enough for today.

Her phone rang, and she didn't recognize the number, but she answered anyway, needing something—anything—to take her mind off the epic disappointment weighing on her chest. "Emily O'Connell."

"Texas Ranger Emily O'Connell?" a soft female voice asked. She recognized hesitation in the woman's tone.

"This is she. And who am I speaking with?"

"Um…my name is Cara Durham. I saw the news article. Rachel Dillingham said I should call you."

"Okay."

"I knew Lexi Bryant. I never thought her death was an accident. Drunk driving. Lexi didn't drink. Ever. Her father was an alcoholic and so was her grandfather. It never sat right, not even with her mom. She questioned the police, but the case was closed and they told her to mourn her daughter and let it go. Then I noticed other deaths, and it was mentioned how families couldn't believe they would kill themselves or take drugs or whatever. I got to thinking I should speak up, but I was too afraid. I'm still afraid."

Emily glanced at the house. Full of ears. Ears she didn't trust. "Cara, if you have information about Lexi, I want to hear it. There's an old bar at the edge of Cedar Springs called the Lone Star." No one would guess she'd choose a bar in a small town to meet. "I'll be there in thirty minutes."

She turned to go inside and Rhode stood at the door. "You're making a mistake, Ranger," he spat out. Then he brushed by her and down the stairs to his truck.

How long had he been there? She grabbed her purse and gun from the entryway and noticed the house was eerily quiet.

A pang of guilt needled her sides, but she left.

She would do this on her own. It was clear she could only trust one person.

Herself.

Stone paced on the back porch; he'd been at it for about an hour and a half now. How could Emily point her finger at him like that? The accusations had been like a billion bees buzzing and stinging. He'd done everything he knew to do to prove she could not only trust in him but depend on him. He'd been patient. Cautious. Quiet when necessary and vocal at other times. He'd brought her into his home, into his family and welcomed her. Made her safe. Put security all around her. Provided her with everything he knew she needed, and yet she was still rejecting him. Rejecting his words. His actions.

His love.

Because he did love her; no point trying to lie to himself. But a chasm divided them. One that at this point couldn't be crossed. She may have severed it forever with her unbelief. He could lay out a solid path to bring them back together, but if she wouldn't walk it, it didn't matter how much he laid down—even his own life—the path was as good as invisible.

But she was right about one thing.

No one knew of their plans and theories but their little makeshift task force.

The front door slammed and Stone came inside as Rhode entered, a backpack slung across his shoulder. "Was it you?" Stone asked. "Just be up front and we can figure it out."

Rhode pushed his long bangs back, but they fell into his eyes again. "Was what me?" he asked.

"Did you tip off PJ after we talked last night? Emily knows. She thinks it's me or you, but either way, I'm responsible, and your behavior has been…shady. You disappear. You get defensive. You refuse to follow facts over feeling. So, I gotta ask. Because I suspect you've been feeding information to the enemy camp."

Rhode's dark eyes narrowed. "Are you serious right now?"

"I am." He hated accusing his brother, but something was up.

Stone inwardly flinched at the glint in Rhode's eyes.

His jaw worked and his nostrils flared. "I've made mistakes. I'm still paying for the consequences of my sins. We can't all be the good son. The perfect one. But I love this family, and I wouldn't have even brought that woman in here. Sissy has been shot. *Shot*. Mama is beside herself, and who can blame her? Bridge isn't sleeping. All of this—it's on you and that piece of work you're in love with. And that love is blinding you. You're the one making mistakes. You're the one turning on your family because she has some kind of daddy issue."

"Do not talk about her like that!"

"No? The woman who you just said accused you of feeding information to the enemy camp? Those were your words. She's certifiable, Stone. Unstable. Biased. Prejudiced—"

"Enough!" Stone bellowed as he got up in Rhode's face. "You don't know anything about her."

He thrust his finger into Stone's face. "Oh, but I do. I know her daddy kept a second family her whole life. And it's affected her, Stone. I know she grew up scraping by, and that prejudices her to wealthy people. I know she has a chip on her shoulder and something to prove. I know that because I recognize that same hunger in her eyes. And it'll be her downfall, and sadly, it's going to be yours too." He leaned back. "Now get out of my way." Rhode stormed by him and headed for Sissy's room.

"Did you feed them information?" Stone asked again.

"No." He didn't even knock on his twin's door. He just went in to her.

Stone pawed his face. Rhode had made some valid points. Emily was biased. She was letting what had torn her up personally affect her job, affect how she felt about him.

It would be the downfall of her if she couldn't reconcile it. He checked her room. Her mother opened the door at his knock. "Is Emily in here?" he asked.

"No. I haven't seen her. Is everything all right?"

"Yeah. Sorry to disturb you." He quietly closed the door and stormed downstairs and out on the front porch, where she was earlier.

Her car was gone. Why would she take off like that? Irresponsible and reckless! He called her cell phone and when he got her voicemail, his heart rate picked up. His chest tightened and he felt flushed in his neck and face.

Where was the woman? And was she safe?

And if Rhode hadn't spilled the beans, who did?

THIRTEEN

Cara Durham sat across from Emily in a back booth, her blue eyes boring into Emily's as she gripped a glass of sweet tea. She'd told Emily how she and Lexi had gone to college together and run with PJ and the boys—minus Rhode Spencer, who didn't attend the same college, but she had known him when he came around in the summers. She'd been in that circle of friends until after Lexi died.

"What happened after Lexi died that you lost touch with your old friends?" Emily asked and sipped her water with lemon.

"I didn't lose touch. I cut ties." She sighed. "Look, the day Lexi had her car accident due to drunk driving, I was with her. All day and into that night. She never had a drop to drink. We'd attended an event at the Pembertons'."

"Royce and Janice Barr-Pemberton?"

"Yes. It was the governor's birthday party."

"Okay. Go on."

"Lexi had worked on the governor's campaign, and during that time, she'd dated PJ. But it didn't take long for her to realize that PJ compared her to Paisley. PJ always had a thing for Paisley."

"I thought PJ was in love with Deidre Dillion?"

"They dated after Paisley died and after things ended with Lexi. I think he might have really wanted a go with her, but no one was Paisley Spencer." She shrugged.

So, PJ had been romantically involved with at least three of the victims.

"Her death rocked him and immortalized her. And Lexi couldn't compete with that, neither could Deidre. PJ was the reason she was there, but he's not who I want to talk about."

"Who do you want to talk about?"

Cara's gaze batted around, then she leaned in. "Royce Pemberton."

Royce?

She wasn't expecting that name to come out of the woman's mouth. Royce Pemberton was squeaky clean. A good man. But then she'd thought that about her father too. "Did you see them?"

"I did. He had her cornered in an alcove, and it was obvious she was upset and wanted to leave, but he had her blocked with his arm and his body. I approached and he let her go. She didn't want to talk about it with me though, and that was so weird. I don't know if he propositioned her or what, but after that, she wanted to get out of there. I took her home. Later that night, they said she died in a drunken car crash. I knew then something was up, but Mr. Pemberton is a powerful man, and I was scared. I had no proof anything had really happened, but that made two of my friends who had either committed suicide or died in an accident."

Emily's mind was working to put pieces in order. "Did you ever tell anyone?"

"No. I was going to, but two days after her accident, I got a call from Royce Pemberton. I never gave him my number. He asked if I could talk with him. It scared me. I said I was going out of town, and I did. I went to South Carolina to visit my aunt for a couple months. Broke off contact with everyone and wouldn't even return their phone calls."

Emily wasn't sure what to think. Royce would have connections too. He was a fraternity brother of the governor. He was appointed by him. He had access to all these same young women. "And you have no idea what he wanted?"

"No." She pushed away her drink. "But looking back, he was always hovering in the background, or he'd be at the lake house when we wanted to hang out, which always surprised Trystan because it wasn't like Royce didn't know we were there. He did. Trystan had to get the house and boat keys from him in advance. I don't know. It was just…unnerving."

Emily let the information process. Could Royce Pemberton be hiding behind his mask of integrity and killing young women? The man was married to a woman who advocated for abused and trafficked women! Emily needed a thorough check run on him. And she knew just who to ask.

"Look, keep yourself scarce and safe. Have you told anyone at all that you're meeting me?"

"No. No one. I know how dangerous this can be. And it might be nothing, but I wish I'd have pressed Lexi and then the issue of her death, but instead I stayed scared and silent. I can't do that anymore."

Emily took her hand and squeezed. "I understand. You go out first, and then I'll leave in about twenty minutes. Just to be safe. But talk to no one else."

She nodded and left. Emily called Rachel Dillingham. Without giving her the information, she told her to see what she could turn up on Royce Pemberton and to be careful, quiet. So far she'd proven she had the skills or contacts with skills to find information.

Emily ordered a basket of fries and let time slip by. When she checked her muted phone, she saw that Stone had called her three times but left no voicemail. She'd flown off the handle and said things she couldn't take back. All her hurt and frustration that deserved to be aimed at her deceased father had been hurled at Stone.

He wasn't a rock that words would bounce off of; he was a man. With flesh and blood and a heart she'd all but shredded.

Damage was done.

No apology was going to make those wrongs right, and she'd apologized so many times before, that it felt shallow anyway. Why couldn't she have just kept her mouth shut?

She ate all her fries, then drowned the rest of her feelings in a milkshake before heading out. But on the way home, she noticed a car keeping about thirty feet behind her. Her pulse spiked.

Was she being followed?

Emily pulled into the ranch, her nerves rattled even though the car had turned off a few roads back. It must have been a coincidence.

Now she had to face Stone.

He may have already packed her bags for her. She wouldn't blame him if he wanted her gone— and her mom too. Emily had brought trouble to him and his family. No denying that. Sissy's gunshot wound was all her fault. And she'd basically spit in all their faces. Stone was dealing with his mother's cancer and so many other burdens, including her own. She entered the house ready to take her lumps and face the music.

The house was extremely loud as she entered. The Chipmunks Christmas album was blaring. What was going on? Stone stepped into the living room from the kitchen, fury in his green eyes. She knew she'd angered him, but not to that degree.

"First off," he said. "You left. You didn't just go blow off steam on the porch. You left. Walked away. You promised me you wouldn't do that. I can't be with a woman who walks away when it's difficult. Won't be. Even if I love her."

He loved her? Is that what he was implying? Her heart slid to her toes.

"Second, no one has been slipping information to anyone." He held up a little black crushed listening device the size of a fingernail. "I've found five so far. Living room. Kitchen. Your bedroom—figured you for a bed maker by the way—the porch and patio. Our phones aren't bugged, but that might just be because we got new phones after our romp in the lake."

Bugged. Someone had come in before he'd installed security and bugged the ranch. No wonder they hadn't been shot at or blown up again. Why when they could follow the investigation by listening? Someone got PJ out of dodge. Why? Was there more than one player involved? Were these murders a group effort?

Cara. She needed Cara to know that someone had overheard her saying she'd meet her at the bar. Emily had felt watched leaving the Lone Star. But no one followed her. What if someone had followed Cara? And Rachel Dillingham? Quickly, she texted each woman to let them know someone had been tipped off about them and to be careful. Stay low. Trust no one.

Bugged. Why hadn't she thought of that? Because it was easier to be mad at the flesh and blood before her. The horrific things she'd hurled at Stone sat like lead in her stomach, and the words she'd said about Rhode.

She couldn't blame her dad for her decision to unload hurtful words. She had let fear rule her actions, but they were hers alone. "I don't know what to say, Stone."

"Sorry is a good start. But it's not going to help us—personally." His eyes softened. "There's too much between us, Em. And after that last stunt… I don't see us patching things up, because I can't trust you to trust me. And you can't trust me. So that's a problem." Pain darkened his eyes and he sighed. "I think I got all the bugs, but Bridge is bringing a device to help us sweep the house."

She nodded. "I'm sorry. I really am and you're

right. There's no fixing what might have been. I take full responsibility for that." She wiped the moisture from her eyes. "I'd like to talk to Rhode." Time to eat crow.

"He's out back, where it's debugged and safe."

She nodded and a thought hit her. What if Rhode bugged the house to throw them off himself? No. No, she had to stop with the paranoia. It had to stop somewhere.

Stepping out on the back deck, she saw him bristle. "*Sorry* doesn't feel like a strong enough word, Rhode." She tiptoed near the sitting area, where he was perched on the wicker couch. The labs slept at his feet.

"May I?" she asked before sitting across from him.

He glanced at her. "Free country."

She eased into the chair. "Truth time?"

"I've been telling the truth," he muttered.

"Maybe I haven't been. Or at least owning up to it." She swallowed her mountain of pride and told him about her father and what it had done to her. "I idolized him. And that was my problem. We can't put anyone on a pedestal, not even family. But I did, and I feel so betrayed, like I just wasn't enough. You know? Like if I'd have been smarter or better or… I don't know. Maybe he would have loved me enough to not need another family. And I've let what I've seen in this job and what happened to me personally wreck everything good in my life. Or what could be good."

Rhode had listened carefully, not interrupting. He held her gaze. "I knew about your dad. I'm a good detective, and something wasn't gelling. I'm sorry too—not for snooping but for misjudging you. I said things behind your back that were out of anger, and I didn't have the whole story. So, I'm sorry and I forgive you."

"You do?" Why would he? That fast?

"I understand on some level how you feel. I get letting things mess up your life and not knowing how to pull yourself up. I don't know how to get it together other than faith and God. But even then it's hard." He gave a sharp laugh. "That word feels so...understated. At one time, I was untrustworthy, and I'm reaping those consequences. Maybe I'm madder at myself than you."

"Who would have thought the one thing we have in common is insecurity?" She laughed and he grinned, dimples creasing the bronze skin of his cheeks.

"We have more than that in common. We both love my brother."

"I don't love—"

"Save it. You do."

"Maybe. But 'sorry' isn't going to fix what I've messed up." And it burned in her gut like a wildfire she couldn't put out.

"Sorry doesn't fix everything. Time might." He shrugged and reached down into his backpack. "I have been working. But I'm not one to unload speculation. And to be honest, I'm having a real hard time thinking one of my lifelong friends or their family members might be a killer. Might have killed my own sister." His voice broke. "I idolized her," he murmured.

Emily had been so focused on her problems she hadn't seen how devastated this family was. At least she hadn't seen past Stone and his pain. "I am sorry."

"I believe you." He hefted the bag onto the couch. "Might as well get Stone out here. Bridge is meeting with his FBI agent friend."

Rhode texted Stone, and in minutes, he moseyed out back with a cup of coffee.

"What's going on?" Stone asked.

"I did my job," Rhode said. "I looked into all the fraternity brothers of Paul Henderson. Most everyone is pretty clean, as in not a murderer or having behavior that points to being one, but something did come up on Royce Pemberton."

Emily's stomach jumped.

Stone leaned in as Rhode spoke.

"I didn't go to private school, so during the school year, I wasn't privy to parties. Only during the summers and Christmas, so I did not know about this," he said firmly. "If I had, I'd have said something. And Trystan's never mentioned it. Ever. Probably from embarrassment."

Emily gave a resolute nod. "I believe you, Rhode."

She just didn't believe Stone. It smarted, but he was glad the fences had been mended between her and his brother.

"Thank you," Rhode said. "Well, as the newspaper tells it, a few of Trystan's friends were spending a weekend at their lake house—parents present. A girl named Vickie Palmetto accidentally fell down the stairs. She was comatose for almost three years, and then she died. According to sources, the Pembertons paid all the hospital bills since it was at their home that the tragedy happened."

Emily's gut twisted. "But?"

"But given the nature of our victims' deaths—homicides appearing like suicides or accidents—I dug deeper. Made some calls. I didn't know some of the kids at the lake house that weekend, but according to them now, they said there was heavy drinking involved, and there were no parents there. But one attendee, Jamie Lee, said that later that night, Trystan's dad showed up acting all surprised to see them there, and Trystan was ticked. He knew better. Jamie said that Royce was talking to Vickie Palmetto before she fell down those stairs."

Emily looked at Stone. "This tracks. This pattern of Royce being at his son's parties or events."

"I can also attest to that," Rhode said. "It would make Trystan so mad."

"Why does it track for you?" Stone asked Emily. He listened as she explained why she left the ranch and who she was meeting.

"I remember Cara. She hasn't been around since Lexi died, but if she's scared of Royce, then it makes sense," Rhode said. He shook his head. "He's always seemed like such a stand-up guy."

"Was PJ at that weekend event?" Stone asked.

Rhode nodded. "So was Beau."

No one had been crossed off the list. The governor, his chief of staff, Beau Brighton, PJ Henderson and now Royce Pemberton. If anything, the pool of suspects had grown. "Can you reach PJ even if he's in Morocco?"

"I tried, but I got his voicemail. I left a message. If he calls, I'll let you know." Rhode shifted in his seat. "I did talk to Beau and he's freaking out. Against legal advice, he talked to me about half an hour ago. I'd have told you earlier, but we found the bugs."

"And?" Stone asked.

"He lied about seeing Deidre the day she died

because he said it was obvious he was looking guilty, and he panicked. His dad already believes he's a delinquent and so does half the world. He didn't know PJ had taken that photo, so when it showed up in the news, he was shocked. He's not leaving the country, but he is laying low at his mansion."

"And what about Talia and the stable and the wallet left behind?" Emily asked.

"He'd gone out to the barn to get away from his dad, who had embarrassed him earlier. He hadn't even been back in town two hours before he started in on him. I heard some of it myself. He said he sat in the hay to get ahold of himself. He never saw the governor or anyone until he left the stable. He met Talia in passing, and then he moved on. He wanted a lawyer because he was probably the last one to see her alive, except for the killer, and he knew how it looked when his wallet had been found at the scene. It must have fallen from his pocket," Rhode said.

Once they saw Talia's texts and who had sent her one right before she went to the stable, it might clear Beau.

"So, why did PJ send the photos of Beau?" Emily asked. "Did he truly want justice? He might believe Beau really did it and his motives aren't nefarious."

Fair enough, Stone thought. "If the governor

isn't behind this, then he may not know what's happening. He could shed some light on things. We could approach him as help, not as a suspect."

Emily nodded. "Let's talk to him at the zoo Christmas Eve event. Super low-key. Just in passing. Make him feel less caged—no pun intended."

At this point, they had nothing left to lose.

Stone left Mama's sitting area. She'd assured him she was feeling better but was simply too tired to attend the event. Sissy was going to stay home with her even though Mama had insisted she needn't bother. Stone wasn't born in a box. Beau would be at the event; his father wouldn't let him escape it now that he was back in town, and wherever Beau was, Sissy made sure she wasn't.

This wasn't how he envisioned Christmas Eve.

He slipped on a navy blue blazer to go with his khaki pants and Timberlands. When he stepped inside the kitchen to meet up with Emily, the tension was thick and uncomfortable.

As hurt and angry as he was, his mouth still turned dry as he drank her in. She wore sleek black jeans and knee-high boots and a long black sweater.

There was too much baggage between them, but that didn't stop the ache in his chest.

She deposited her gun in her handbag. "I haven't checked the weather. Will I need a coat?"

"Nah. Unless you're prone to being cold. Low sixties. Merry Christmas Eve." Nothing about it felt merry.

"I may take one just in case. Where are your brothers?"

"Rhode went ahead of us. Is your mom coming?"

Emily unwrapped a piece of gum. "No, she's going to a church service with her friends and back to one of their houses for a late dinner. She said she should be home by eleven." She tossed the wrapper in the trash. "I can't tell her she can't go to church or enjoy a holiday with her friends. I was tempted to though."

"I hear ya. But we can't all go into hiding and hope it blows over. It won't. Not unless we finish what we've started." Stone pocketed his wallet. "Ready?"

"Yeah."

They took her car the forty minutes to the old zoo that was now a park. Tree branches held strings of white lights and bows. A huge white tent had been set up with a bar, and there was food outside the old entrance. A new wrought iron fence read Old Zoo Hiking Trails. The decor didn't really fix the eerie sensation of an old abandoned zoo.

"It's not too holly or jolly," Stone said, even though Johnny Mathis was singing his heart out otherwise. They entered the gate, handed their tickets to the woman and moved into the crowd of people. "Who thought it was a good idea to plant a zoo in the middle of the woods?"

"All I see is assaults in these hidden places. I hope women won't hike these trails alone. And I hate that I have to say that. Men never have to worry about hiking alone." She harrumphed.

He concurred. The double standard was unfortunate. "Let's check out the place and see who we see."

They walked a hiking path that curved around a man-made cave that had once been a lion's den.

Up ahead, he saw the governor. "It's time."

Paul spotted Stone and waved. He probably had protective duty nearby, but they were blending in well.

"Good to see you," Paul said when they approached. "And you again, Ranger O'Connell. I actually planned to call you after the holidays."

"What about?" Emily asked.

They walked off the main hiking path into what might have been a bear's enclosure. "I've read the news. Heard the gossip. Seen the implications that Beau Brighton might be responsible for these possible homicides. I don't believe it—

not that the accidents and suicides were staged, but that it could be Beau."

"Who do you think it could be?"

Paul smirked. "I don't know. But I suspect you are looking right at me."

"Why would you think that?" Emily asked.

"Because I would be. I appreciate you being discreet. Had you not been, this conversation might not have been quite so cordial."

They'd been right not to come at him and to keep it quiet. The last thing Stone needed was lawsuits filed against him and Emily could lose her job. "Well, we do have questions, and we thought chatting here might not give people the impression we're discussing a case. What can you tell us about the victims? How well did you know them?"

Paul sighed. "Between us, I knew Deidre and Talia intimately. The other women were family friends or had something to do with work. That's it. I promise."

"Why did PJ leave the country?" Emily asked.

Paul shook his head. "I don't know why PJ does what PJ does. I didn't even know he left until my wife told me. Do you think he has something to do with these deaths?" His eyes held skepticism.

"We know he leaked the photos of Beau, and

they're best friends. Why would he do that?" Emily asked.

"Maybe he thinks Beau did it. I do not. I didn't. And I don't think my son did either, but his bolting doesn't exactly cast him in a positive light." The scowl revealed he was thoroughly displeased with his son. "I want to help you find the truth. These women were related to or close to my fraternity brothers. We're family. What can I do?"

Helping them meant he would have direct access to the investigation. Stone didn't like that, and he knew Emily wouldn't either. "You could provide alibis for the nights each woman died."

Paul ran his tongue across his teeth. "Of course. Martin keeps…" His voice trailed off. Was he suspecting Martin of framing him as they'd earlier believed? "Martin keeps my calendar. I'll have him email you where I was. Though I know I was with Deidre the night she died. She'd come to the party to see me, but I had other plans for later that night, and we got into an argument about that. She left and I didn't see her again."

"These other plans… Were they with a woman?"

"Yes, my wife. We'd been trying to reconnect. Get back the old spark."

Clearly, that had failed. His wife was a lousy

alibi. "If you could get PJ back home to talk with us, we'd love that."

"I'll try."

A group of men called his name, and he waved. "I'll be in touch," he told Stone and Emily as he left to meet up with the men.

"So Deidre had been with Beau earlier the day of her death, then gone to the party to see the governor. Was Royce Pemberton at that party?" Emily asked.

"Likely."

"I have another theory. Could Martin Landers and PJ Henderson be in on this together to frame the governor?"

"Explain."

"Martin knew his wife was having an affair with Paul. And PJ knew his father was too. They both had motive to set him up, and throwing out that photo of Beau and Deidre was perfect. As they suspected, it wouldn't look like he was framing his father if he was a suspect."

Good points. "But why leave? Why not stay and put the final nail in his father's coffin?" A piece of the puzzle wasn't fitting.

"Maybe he got scared and took off, thinking we might be on to him. And Martin couldn't leave. Not with Talia having just passed, or it would look suspicious."

"It's possible."

"We still need to talk to Royce Pemberton. I want to know about the girl who fell down his stairs and hear his answers to Cara Durham's statement concerning Lexi Bryant."

"And we will."

Emily's phone rang. "It's Bridge." She answered. "Hello."

Her face paled. "What? When?… He's here with me… Yes, I'll tell him." She ended the call.

"Is it your mom? My mom?"

She shook her head. "Cara Durham's dead."

FOURTEEN

Emily stared at her phone. She'd warned Cara, but it had done no good. Someone had taken her out. Now there was no witness to testify if they ever went to trial. And the only one who had anything to gain was Royce Pemberton.

"This is my fault." Cara's blood was on Emily's hands.

"No," Stone said and laid a firm hand on her shoulder. "You had no idea the ranch was bugged. None of us did, and when you found out, you texted her. You can't blame yourself."

But she did. "It's just a bunch of hearsay about Royce now. Unless we can find someone else who might know something. His wife? If he's untoward to young girls, wouldn't she have an idea?" She shook her head. "No. Most people assume women are lying about not having any clue to their husband's nefarious behavior. I used to be one. Except it was my father and me, and

Mom had no idea he was living another life. And we are not naive, stupid people."

She shivered even though she wasn't cold. "Would his son offer anything up?"

"Doubtful if Trystan knows anything. They have a decent relationship, unlike Beau with his father. Or even PJ, who might want to see his father burn for all the betrayal. Or we're dealing with more than one of them working together, but for what common goal? Maybe someone or several people are being blackmailed into helping."

Stone's phone rang and he frowned. "It's Sissy."

He answered and Emily whispered, "I'm going to go get us hot chocolates."

Plus, she needed a minute to process the fact that Cara was now dead. Supposedly, she'd had a car accident after leaving the bar. Emily knew better. But whoever was in the killer's pocket in Cedar Springs would remove any suspicion in their reports. Poor Cara. All she'd tried to do was help Emily stop a killer.

A killer... If the killer went as far back as the death of the girl at the weekend house when the boys were in high school, then there was no known motive. And there might be more accidents. They'd been looking into women who connected to the governor. But they needed to look at girls, and women, who connected to Royce Pemberton.

She stepped up to the drink bar and picked up two hot chocolates.

"Nice night for a grand opening." Royce Pemberton moseyed up to Emily.

He'd been at his wife's office the day she and Stone had interviewed her. He could have easily had someone run them off the road, keep them from digging into the homicides with one phone call. He had money and power and a perfect shield to hide behind—chair of the ethics committee.

"Yeah." Emily scanned him. Dressed impeccably. Attractive. Kind eyes.

"Any new updates on the case?"

"No," she said coolly, but inside she was wound tight. "What might you know about these young women? Anything to give me insight?"

"Me?" He picked up one hot chocolate, and they walked away from the booth. "It's hard to believe someone would be killing women and staging their deaths to mask homicides. I don't particularly like the timing of PJ's trip to a place where he can't be extradited. Might chase that angle."

"We definitely are." She blew on her hot chocolate. "Lexi worked for you, didn't she?"

"For a while. Sweet girl." He paused midsip. "You're not hovering over the idea that I'm involved, are you?"

Now or never. Time to squeeze the trigger. "Well, it's come to my attention a girl had an accident at your home over a decade ago. Fell down the stairs. Kind of fits in with these other accidents now."

He lowered his cup of hot chocolate. "Tread lightly, Ranger O'Connell. That was a tragic accident. Nothing more."

"Just seems odd is all." She sipped her drink but had no taste for it. "I'd love your alibis for the nights these women died. You don't mind, do you?"

His jaw hardened. "Not at all. I'll pull my calendar and let you know."

"I appreciate it."

"I don't want to hold up justice."

She wasn't buying it.

He held up his drink. "Enjoy the night and be careful, Ranger O'Connell. You're just one woman. And it seems women end up dying." He waltzed off before she could respond to what she perceived as a threat.

Now where was Stone? His drink was going to get cold. She wandered through the crowd and past the former animal exhibits as her thoughts rolled around her head and she tried to make pieces fit. She approached the old bear's den, where a gate hung open.

"Someone poisoned the bear, you know. Back

in the seventies. Weird." Trystan Pemberton approached and pointed to the bear cave. "Then a lion died. Guess they cut their losses and got out before it became worse."

Emily considered the history. "No one investigated?"

"No one cared. Or maybe they didn't want the publicity of someone murdering animals. That would be…unethical." Trystan held her gaze, and Emily read between the lines. He was giving her something on Royce without directly giving her something.

"What happened that night at the lake house with Vickie Palmetto?" she asked.

Trystan's dark blue eyes dulled and his mouth pinched. "I wish that night had never happened," he mumbled and began walking away as if trying to slowly escape the memory.

Emily followed.

"We were all just blowing off steam. It was supposed to be a weekend study group and we did a little studying at first. Me, PJ, Beau, Vickie, Jamie Lee and a couple of other girls."

"Did you know your dad was going to be there?" she asked as they wound around the hiking trail, the tree limbs creating a canopy.

"No. But he knew we were. I had to get a key from my mom. I usually bypassed him. He… hovered."

Same thing Cara had said when talking about Royce and Lexi Bryant in the later college years. Maybe she'd just take a chance and ask what they both seemed to be dancing around. "Do you think your dad had anything to do with the deaths of Vickie, Paisley, Lexi, Deidre and Tiffany? Even Talia?"

Trystan adjusted his gray blazer. "Do you?" he asked as they approached a rocky crag. Double dens had been carved into the hills. "That's the wolf den. Me and dad always loved the wolves best. Once on a trip to Alaska he took me to a wolf sanctuary. It was awesome." He stepped closer to the dens. "Dad was obsessed with them. Wanted a wolf dog."

Emily remained where she was. Royce Pemberton might love wolves because he was one. In sheep's clothing. "If he did, it doesn't explain why PJ would jump ship to a place where he can't be extradited. You know anything about that? Heard from PJ?"

"Nah." Trystan ran his hand along the den. "Maybe it's not about the governor at all. If you're locked on that, you're missing something else. My dad forced me to take criminal law classes. That's kind of 101." He shrugged. "And maybe PJ thinks he's a suspect and has never had the spine to take conflict head-on. He likes to stir the pot, but he never can take the heat if it gets too hot. And I'd say this is pretty hot. The fact that he bolted means nothing. He bolted when Vickie fell down the stairs too. Literally said, 'I'm out of here.' And he was. Didn't even stick around to offer comfort to his then flavor of the week."

Trystan had a point.

He leaned into the den and pushed out a breath as he backed up. He curled his lip. "It still smells like animal in there. How can that be?" He waved his hand in front of his face. "Dude, it's like something died in there."

Emily's pulse spiked. "Hold on." She moved toward the den, and together they stepped inside.

Trystan let out a cry and stumbled backward falling on his behind. "There's a body in here! It's a woman. A dead woman!"

Stone ended the call with Sissy. Mama had passed out, and Sissy had called an ambulance. Stone's blood whooshed in his ears, and his neck and face flushed. He checked his fitness watch. His heart rate was way up, which probably meant his blood pressure was too.

God, why is so much happening at once? He could use a break. A reprieve. Something. Anything. Why when it rained did it pour? Was he being punished or something? Had God forgotten his faithfulness?

A hand on his shoulder startled him.

"Bruh, what's got you wound up like a spring?" Beau Brighton stood with a scowl on his face.

"Nothing. Everything. Have you seen Ranger O'Connell?"

"She's hard to miss. She's hot."

Stone *was* wound as tight as a coil, and he didn't need Beau's comment. "One more word…"

Beau grinned. "Stone, I'm just saying. She's a pretty lady, and no, I haven't seen her." He cleared his throat. "Have you seen Sissy tonight? I figured she'd be here. Just wanted to see that she's doing okay. Rhode said she's recovering. I doubt she'd accept my visit or flowers, so…" He shrugged one shoulder.

Stone heard the hesitancy and sincerity in Beau's voice. "She's recovering well. She stayed with Mama tonight. But…" Might as well tell the tale; he'd already had to tell Sissy under duress—not the way he planned. He hadn't told his brothers though, so he refrained.

"But what?" His bright eyes widened. "Is she okay? She hurt?"

"No. Sissy's fine. It's nothing. Have you seen Rhode?"

"Not in a minute." Beau scratched the back of his head. "You still looking at me as a suspect?"

"Should I?"

"Probably. But I didn't do it. I called PJ. Talked to him."

Maybe he should have led with that. "And?"

Beau pinched the bridge of his nose. "I told him I know why he sent the photos. He thought I committed the murders, and his distrust goes back to the time I took Pai to the Bahamas. There was never anything romantic between us. I'd never do that to Sissy. Never."

"No, you'd just betray her in other ways."

Beau's lips tightened. "I never said I was a stand-up guy. But I care about Sissy and I always have."

Stone snorted. "Horrible way to show it."

"Paisley needed a break. She was wound tight—a lot like you right now. So, I made her go with me for the weekend. We had fun. Legal nonromantic fun and it worked. She loosened up. Felt better about her job. And that was that. PJ never believed it was anything platonic, and I can't blame him for that. I'm rarely platonic with a woman, and that includes Deidre. Yeah, I knew her more than I let on, in a way that PJ didn't like." He had the decency to blush and look away. "He sent the photos to call me out and humiliate me. We're friends, but he's always been jealous of me."

"You need better friends."

"I have better friends, but PJ and I grew up together. Things like that don't change."

"Why'd he leave?"

Beau shoved his hands in his jeans pockets. "Thought I might come after him. Accidents are happening. There's buzz all over. I think I convinced him I'm not the killer, but who knows? He didn't do it. But he's not coming home until whoever did is caught. He's not exactly one who loves confrontation or conflict. Why do you think he follows in his dad's footsteps? He's too afraid to say he doesn't want to go into politics."

Stone nodded and scanned the area. Where was Emily? He couldn't stick around much longer. He needed to get to the hospital ASAP. Any further questioning would have to wait. He turned back to tell Beau when he spotted Royce near the trees talking to his wife.

"Stone," Beau said, calling back his attention, "I'm not the best man for advice or really anything, but you look like you have the weight of the world on you. And I've been in your family long enough to know that your faith is in God. Not you. So whatever has your face red and in a perpetual squint…maybe put it in the faith box or whatever. You're one man."

Stone opened his mouth to debate, but Beau had made some sense. Stone was one man. Bearing burdens that weren't his. Now, if he could just find that box or whatever. "My mom is sick."

And he spilled his guts to Beau Brighton—the billionaire brat of Texas.

"I'm real sorry, bro. I love Miss Marisol like my own mama." Beau gave him a man hug. "We need to find Rhode and the ranger, and get y'all to the hospital."

"You come with us."

Beau smiled, but it was sad. "Nah, Sissy wouldn't like that."

"Sissy needs to get over whatever it was that went down between the two of you," Stone said, but agreed they needed to find Rhode and Emily.

"Sissy is well within her rights to never speak to me again. I don't blame her. You shouldn't either. I'll hunt for Rhode. You find the redhead." Beau darted off, and Stone went on the search for Emily.

Where was Royce? He'd been by the trees a few minutes ago.

Now he was gone.

FIFTEEN

Emily rushed into the wolves' den, tripped over something that felt like a foot and fell to the dirty musk-scented ground.

The empty ground.

No body.

Suddenly, Trystan was on her, elbowing her in the face and shoving a tiny pill into her mouth. She worked to spit it out, but he had her arms gripped with one hand and her mouth shut with the other. She would not swallow it.

But her pulse spiked as it dawned on her that the pill was quickly dissolving.

No. No. No.

Her eyes widened as it completely dissolved.

Trystan smiled. "Good girl."

Emily's body became languid, and he must have felt it too because he removed his hand from her mouth.

"You?" she whispered as her body turned to water and her brain clouded.

"All me." He dragged her farther into the den, into the dark. "Vickie was an accident. I wanted to go further than her in our…relationship, but she fought. I didn't mean to push her down the stairs. I grabbed at her to get her to remain upstairs with me. But she fell. Now, looking back, maybe I did mean to push her, because once she landed, it was…incredible. The rush of power. I did that. I caused that. I had her life in my hands, and I let it go."

"You're sick."

"Maybe," he said smugly. "I was scared though. I thought I was in serious trouble. Dad came out of the library and saw her. His panicked face was priceless. I don't think he ever believed it was an accident. He caught me once before that. With a cat."

Emily winced, and her head began to swirl into oblivion.

He ran his finger down her cheek as he squatted over her. "I figure that's why he took care of the medical bills their insurance didn't cover—guilt. And that he believed it was the right thing to do. Deep down, he knew what his son was."

A serial killer. A sociopath.

"And he monitored me. Hovering over my friends and always being where I was. It infuriated me. He even tried to talk Lexi Bryant out of going on a trip with me once. Didn't save her in the end though. Probably saved Cara for awhile."

"You had her killed for talking with me, but she thought your dad was the one. Why kill her at all? Who's in your pocket?" Her words slurred as her mind muddied. "Who did you pay off? How?"

"Oh, me?" Trystan laughed. "I did no such thing. I don't care if the police know they were murdered." He leaned into her ear, but she had no strength to push him away. Not even when he placed a soft kiss on her lobe. "I suffocated them. Just like I'll suffocate you." He covered her nose and mouth to get his point across. "And I'll get away with it like I always have."

She tried to fight for air, but she felt so sleepy.

"What is going on in here?" a deep voice boomed.

Emily slowly swung her groggy gaze to the entrance of the den as Trystan let her go. She gasped as she saw light surround Royce Pemberton. "What have you done to her?"

"Nothing." Trystan chuckled. "Yet. And you and mommy will clean it all up and hide it like you've been doing. Because forbid it all a Pemberton might be something other than upstanding, good and kind."

Royce's brow furrowed. "I haven't covered up anything you've done, and neither has your mother. I didn't know you'd done any of this!"

Even in her haze, Emily couldn't believe him. He must have suspected. He expressed interest in the case, saw Trystan's dark side early on. That's why he'd wanted to talk to Cara about Trystan. It had been too late for Lexi, and he probably had tried to redirect Vickie too.

"Don't lie, Dad. It's not *ethical*." He turned Emily's face to his, her eyes growing even heavier. "See, that's the thing. When I pushed Vickie, I got away with it. Not even a slap on the wrist. And I thought, 'What else can I get away with?' So I did it again. And again. And again. No consequences. The world is mine."

"Is that what you think?" Royce asked, his tone horrified. "You think we were—that I was cleaning up your messes? I wasn't. And I won't. You will pay for every murder and every vicious thing you've done."

"No. He won't," said a female voice.

Janice Barr-Pemberton entered the enclosure.

"Janice?" Royce asked, his voice shocked once again.

"We've worked too hard and long to build our reputation and businesses. I won't see it all crumble. I won't lose it." She held a gun with a silencer on the end.

Royce gawked at his wife. "You've been covering this all up? For Trystan?"

"For all of us. The ME. Detective Lang in

Cedar Springs. As well as a few homicide detectives in Austin. It was easy to buy them off. I hated that it pointed to Beau awhile, thanks to whatever game PJ was playing. But the evidence points to Paul Henderson. He's disgusting, and if he goes down, then he gets what he deserves for his cheating!"

Royce raked a trembling hand through his hair. "Do you hear yourself? You're allowing Trystan to murder innocent women by covering it up and paying people off. I really don't think you can judge Paul Henderson for his affairs." He paced. "What are we going to do?" His voice cracked as his whole world fell apart within seconds.

Welcome to the broken club, Royce.

"We're going to walk away," Janice said evenly. She nodded toward Emily. "She can't live. And when it's done, I'll have it covered up. I have people I pay to do those things."

"People you paid to run her and Stone off the road? All these attacks they've endured?"

Janice huffed. "The dark web will get you anyone or anything you like. As long as you pay."

Even through her haze, Emily was able to piece it together. It hadn't been Trystan trying to kill her. Those attempts had been at the direct order of Janice Barr-Pemberton.

"And Talia?" she managed to ask, trying with all her might to hang on. To stay awake, to get enough strength in her to reach for her handbag and grab her gun.

"I always liked her," Trystan said with a wolfish grin. The perfect place for him was right here inside this wolf den. "Hey, Ma, did a horse kick Talia in the head? How did you get a dark web guy out there so quick?"

Janice pursed her lips. "That one I had to do myself. There was no time to call in any help. Just like I took the opportunity to get rid of Ranger O'Connell. However, it backfired and Stone dragged her from the pool."

Royce put the heels of his hands to his eyes. "How can this be happening? I should have known. No. We will not keep letting this happen. Trystan must pay for his crimes and... Janice..." His voice broke. "When did money ever mean anything to us?"

Janice's laugh was loud and humorless. "I suppose to someone who was never without it, never. But I grew up poor. You know this. A nobody. Now, I'm a somebody."

Royce just stood there and gawked. He had no words.

"If you won't follow the game plan, then you can't be on the team, Royce. I love you. But I won't go back to the poorhouse. I like my life."

Janice pulled the trigger and Royce crumpled to the ground, his shirt seeping with blood.

* * *

Stone had searched the crowd, the food vendors and now was making his way through the hiking trails that looped around the former zoo enclosures, sweat beading his forehead and blood pressure skyrocketing. Where was Emily? Where was Royce? Did he have her?

She wouldn't wander off, and she would at least answer her phone. But it was going straight to voicemail. He passed the bear enclosure, and as he hurried around the ascending trail near the wolves' den, he saw a flash of light, like gun with a muzzle firing in the dark.

Emily!

Stone's blood pressure rose, pounding in his head, and everything sounded like cotton in his ears. Barreling past the gate, he bolted inside, gun in hand and halted upon entry. Janice Barr-Pemberton stood with her back facing him as she stood over Royce, who was lying in a pool of blood. Trystan was straddling Emily, his gloved hand over her nose and mouth.

His whole world slanted but he had to act. Now.

"Drop the gun," he commanded as he aimed his weapon at Janice. "Trystan, let go and get off of Ranger O'Connell. This instant."

Trystan complied, hands up but a smile on his face as he slowly moved off Emily. "Doesn't matter now anyway. She's gone. Just a little overkill," he teased, and Stone restrained from aiming and pulling the trigger on him. Emily was pale. Unmoving.

"Janice, drop the gun."

She didn't budge. "I will not." The gun was still aimed at her husband.

"Janice, you do good work for hurt women. How could you let your son hurt women?"

Inhaling sharply, she raised her chin. "I don't condone it. But I can't put my only son in prison and have a scandal. I've put him in programs. I've sent him overseas. I gave him everything in hopes it would be enough."

There would likely be a trail of murders wherever Janice had sent Trystan. Bloodthirst was never satiated. Serial killers couldn't stop.

"What am I supposed to do?" she asked. "Let our family fall from grace? Become pariahs. No. I worked too hard for this family, this life. I thought maybe he'd be done after the next one."

Stone couldn't believe the words coming out of her mouth. She was as delusional as her son. "How did you know he was behind the murders?"

"I pay to know what my son is doing."

"She's been having me tailed. I know about them. They come in when I'm done and clean it up," Trystan said.

"Or finish the job. You left Tiffany alive." Janice had the nerve to look put out.

But that explained the stool and vanity table items knocked over. The cleaner hadn't had time to finish his cover-up because Judge came home early, and he had to get out of the house, leaving a trail of questions and evidence behind. It also explained why there had been blood spatter, but not the right amount for suicide. He'd shot her only minutes after Trystan left.

These women trusted and knew Trystan. They would let him in their home and not suspect him. Then someone else would come along and stage it all. Clean up a struggle—unless he'd dosed them with something.

"I even hoped he'd turn his sights on women who no one cares about," Janice continued, "like prostitutes."

"I care about them. Janice, they're still people." She was supposed to champion the marginalized women. How could she say that?

"But it's so much more fun," Trystan said, "hunting among Mom and Dad's elite."

Stone's fury bubbled. "Shut up." He knelt and checked Royce's pulse while keeping his eyes on both Janice and Trystan. The man had a faint heartbeat, but without medical attention, he'd be gone soon. Stone was too far away to check for Emily's pulse. "Put that gun down, Janice. It's over."

"I won't go to jail."

"Yeah. You will."

As Stone stood, Janice aimed the gun at her head and pulled the trigger. Stone winced as despair clung to his insides.

Trystan sat quietly. Not even a gasp.

Stone knew there was nothing he could do for Janice Barr-Pemberton now. Training his gun on Trystan, he pulled out his phone and called 911. Then he went to Trystan. "Face on the ground. Hands behind your back. Move slow."

Trystan moved to raise his hands in surrender, but as they ascended from the ground, he was holding a gun. Emily's gun.

In one motion he aimed and fired.

Stone was faster.

Trystan's shot missed.

Stone's didn't.

Trystan fell to the ground, howling in pain and clutching his leg. Stone snatched the gun and shoved it in his waistband, then checked Emily's pulse.

She was alive!

"Kill me!" Trystan wailed. "I'd rather die."

"No, you don't get off that easily." Stone ground his teeth.

It was over.

Finally.

SIXTEEN

Emily blinked open her eyes, her vision slowly focusing. Stone sat on the edge of the couch. How had she gotten here to the ranch? Last she remembered, she was in the wolves' den with Trystan Pemberton. "What happened?"

"First," Stone said as he leaned down and kissed her forehead, "Merry Christmas."

She half laughed. Then her memory surfaced in waves. She'd been put in an ambulance, taken to the hospital. Trystan had given her some kind of drug, and after it wore off and she was in the clear, Stone had brought her back to the ranch, where she'd fallen asleep again.

"Doc said you might have memory loss of the past few hours. What do you last remember?"

"I remember Trystan giving me a pill that dissolved in my mouth. That's about it."

Stone filled her in on what had transpired in the wolves' den.

"Janice shot her own husband?" Emily asked.

"Yeah. Guess she wanted fame and glory more than family, but he did survive."

"The ME and Detective Lang with the Cedar Springs PD have been taken into custody. They'll be doing a more thorough investigation—or you will. It's your unit working the case in tandem with a federal corruption task force. Who knows everyone she paid off? They've taken her laptop and devices, hoping to find the man she hired on the dark web. But we may never find him. Janice probably had him write the threatening notes and take the photo of your mom, who has been worried sick about you by the way, along with the rest of us."

Emily smiled. "So, it's over."

"The danger, yes." He smirked and brushed hair from her face. "Now, I'd like to talk to you about tacos and guacamole."

She laughed. "Yes."

"Yes, you'd like to have a conversation?"

"Yes, I want to have dinner with you." She held his hand. "I should have gone the last two times you asked. I'm stubborn."

He feigned shock. "No. Not you."

She licked her lips, and he handed her a glass of water. She sipped and scooched up on the couch. "I let my fear and my pain over Dad's betrayal mess with how I felt about you. About everyone trying to help me. I can't take back the words I said that I didn't mean. But maybe I can help mend it with new words I do mean."

"Words like tacos and guac?" he asked, but she heard the thick emotion in his voice.

She kissed his hand she was holding. "No. Words like 'I love you,' Stone. I want to love you. And I trust you. I really do."

He framed her face as he searched her eyes. "I believe you," he murmured and descended on her lips, giving her the best Christmas gift she could ever imagine. She pulled him closer as she slowly savored this glorious present.

When he finally broke the kiss, he whispered, "I love you too."

"Well, that would put a real damper on our relationship if you didn't."

He laughed. "I suppose it would." His expression sobered. "You scared me so bad when I saw you lying there and I couldn't tell if you were alive or…not. All I could think about was the timing is never right. We'll always have some kind of baggage or full plate or difficult circumstance. But I want you, and I was planning on convincing you no matter what it took, but you made it a lot easier than I anticipated."

"I'm pretty easy to get along with."

"Well, that's a complete lie," he said through a soft chuckle. "But I wouldn't have you any other way. I have one more gift for you. I teetered on the idea, but after our conversation earlier in the week, I thought...yeah. You trust me?"

"I said I did." She leaned over and kissed him again.

"Then here's another Christmas surprise." He stood and peeked out of the living room.

Her mom entered, tears in her eyes.

A beautiful gift, but she was already here anyway.

"Honey, I was so worried."

"I'm fine." She let her mom hug her and held tight. "You are a wonderful gift to see after all that."

"I'm not your gift, honey. But Stone and I had a conversation, and, well..." She nodded and Stone waved toward the hall. A woman with red hair, dark brown eyes and no freckles entered the room with a measure of hesitancy on her face. Emily knew this woman was her half sister. One she planned to get to know after the investigation closed and it was safe.

"Hi. I'm Dottie. I almost said no about flying in from Oklahoma, but then your mother convinced me."

Her mom. How wonderful.

"And it's hard to say no to your boyfriend."

Boyfriend? She supposed that was what Stone was to her. But she hoped it would be more. Someday.

"He's a bullheaded pig."

Dottie laughed. "He said you'd say that about him."

Stone winked at Emily and her heart took flight. She really did love this man. "Where is your family?" she asked Dottie.

"Home. They understood. My brother couldn't fly out, but he's planning to soon if that's okay."

"Yes." She held out her arms, and Dottie leaned down and hugged her. "I'm so glad to have a sister. I prayed for one my whole life. I had no idea God would answer that prayer."

It seemed God often answered prayers through pain.

"I'm so glad He did. We have a lot of catching up to do."

"That we do."

One by one, the Spencers entered the room, followed by Marisol looking pale and tired.

Stone took her hand, snuggled in beside her and kissed her temple. "We'll talk later."

"I have everyone I care about and those who I know I will come to care for here with me," Marisol said. "It's a beautiful Christmas."

That it was.

"Your mom has been helping with brunch, and it's our tradition to read about the birth of our Savior before we open presents and eat." She held out the Bible for Stone to take and read. He accepted it but paused, then held the Bible out to Rhode.

"Would you do the honors?" he asked.

Rhode's mouth dropped open, but he accepted the Bible. "But you always do it."

"I'm learning I don't have to always do everything."

Rhode opened the black leather-bound Bible and began reading the story from the book of Luke.

Underneath the blanket, Stone took Emily's hand, rubbing her left ring finger. He whispered into her ear, "When's your birthday?"

"April."

"Good. I know just what to get you."

Her heart fluttered and she snuggled against him, her head resting on his chest. She'd always wanted a big family. A big Christmas. And God had blessed her with one.

She couldn't ask for anything more.

Except maybe that ring before April.

* * * * *

Watch for more books in Jessica R. Patch's Texas Crime Scene Cleaners miniseries, coming in 2024 from Love Inspired Suspense!

Dear Reader,

Emily's mistrust of Stone over and over again might have felt over the top. Maybe you, like me when writing, thought: *It's clear he can be trusted. Can't you see?* He made a safe place for her, protected her and even was willing to die for her, and yet she often blamed him and projected her pain onto him. We can see how silly she was. But then I had to take the finger I was pointing at Emily and turn it on myself.

How often do I blame God when things are scary or uncertain? How often do I try to depend on myself and push Him away? How silly that must look, how over the top. He has proven He can be trusted in the sacrificial love and death of Jesus. Maybe you too need to step back and ask God where you've not been giving Him full trust and blaming Him for others' betrayals and for the pain others have caused. We can fully and always trust God.

I love to connect with readers and the best way to do that is through my monthly newsletter. Please sign up and get "Patched In" at JessicaRPatch.com and follow me on BookBub @jessicarpatch.

Warmly,
Jessica

Get 3 FREE REWARDS!

We'll send you 2 FREE Books plus a FREE Mystery Gift.

FREE Value Over **$20**

Both the **Love Inspired®** and **Love Inspired® Suspense** series feature compelling novels filled with inspirational romance, faith, forgiveness and hope.

Get 3 FREE REWARDS!

We'll send you 2 FREE Books plus a FREE Mystery Gift.

FREE
Value Over
$20

Both the **Harlequin® Special Edition** and **Harlequin® Heartwarming™** series feature compelling novels filled with stories of love and strength where the bonds of friendship, family and community unite.

YES! Please send me 2 FREE novels from the Harlequin Special Edition or Harlequin Heartwarming series and my FREE Gift (gift is worth about $10 retail). After receiving them, if I don't wish to receive any more books, I can return the shipping statement marked "cancel." If I don't cancel, I will receive 6 brand-new Harlequin Special Edition books every month and be billed just $5.49 each in the U.S. or $6.24 each in Canada, a savings of at least 12% off the cover price, or 4 brand-new Harlequin Heartwarming Larger-Print books every month and be billed just $6.24 each in the U.S. or $6.74 each in Canada, a savings of at least 19% off the cover price. It's quite a bargain! Shipping and handling is just 50¢ per book in the U.S. and $1.25 per book in Canada.* I understand that accepting the 2 free books and gift places me under no obligation to buy anything. I can always return a shipment and cancel at any time by calling the number below. The free books and gift are mine to keep no matter what I decide.

Choose one: ☐ **Harlequin**
Special Edition
(235/335 BPA GRMK)

☐ **Harlequin**
Heartwarming
Larger-Print
(161/361 BPA GRMK)

☐ **Or Try Both!**
(235/335 & 161/361
BPA GRPZ)

Name (please print)

Address   Apt. #

City   State/Province   Zip/Postal Code

Email: Please check this box ☐ if you would like to receive newsletters and promotional emails from Harlequin Enterprises ULC and its affiliates. You can unsubscribe anytime.

Mail to the **Harlequin Reader Service:**
IN U.S.A.: P.O. Box 1341, Buffalo, NY 14240-8531
IN CANADA: P.O. Box 603, Fort Erie, Ontario L2A 5X3

Want to try 2 free books from another series? Call 1-800-873-8635 or visit www.ReaderService.com.

*Terms and prices subject to change without notice. Prices do not include sales taxes, which will be charged (if applicable) based on your state or country of residence. Canadian residents will be charged applicable taxes. Offer not valid in Quebec. This offer is limited to one order per household. Books received may not be as shown. Not valid for current subscribers to the Harlequin Special Edition or Harlequin Heartwarming series. All orders subject to approval. Credit or debit balances in a customer's account(s) may be offset by any other outstanding balance owed by or to the customer. Please allow 4 to 6 weeks for delivery. Offer available while quantities last.

Your Privacy—Your information is being collected by Harlequin Enterprises ULC, operating as Harlequin Reader Service. For a complete summary of the information we collect, how we use this information and to whom it is disclosed, please visit our privacy notice located at corporate.harlequin.com/privacy-notice. From time to time we may also exchange your personal information with reputable third parties. If you wish to opt out of this sharing of your personal information, please visit readerservice.com/consumerschoice or call 1-800-873-8635. **Notice to California Residents**—Under California law, you have specific rights to control and access your data. For more information on these rights and how to exercise them, visit corporate.harlequin.com/california-privacy.

HSEHW23

Get 3 FREE REWARDS!

We'll send you 2 FREE Books plus a FREE Mystery Gift.

FREE
Value Over
$20

Both the **Mystery Library** and **Essential Suspense** series feature compelling novels filled with gripping mysteries, edge-of-your-seat thrillers and heart-stopping romantic suspense stories.

YES! Please send me 2 FREE novels from the Mystery Library or Essential Suspense Collection and my FREE Gift (gift is worth about $10 retail). After receiving them, if I don't wish to receive any more books, I can return the shipping statement marked "cancel." If I don't cancel, I will receive 4 brand-new Mystery Library books every month and be billed just $6.74 each in the U.S. or $7.24 in Canada, a savings of at least 25% off the cover price, or 4 brand-new Essential Suspense books every month and be billed just $7.49 each in the U.S. or $7.74 each in Canada, a savings of at least 17% off the cover price. It's quite a bargain! Shipping and handling is just 50¢ per book in the U.S. and $1.25 per book in Canada.* I understand that accepting the 2 free books and gift places me under no obligation to buy anything. I can always return a shipment and cancel at any time by calling the number below. The free books and gift are mine to keep no matter what I decide.

Choose one: ☐ **Mystery Library**   ☐ **Essential**   ☐ **Or Try Both!**
                          (414/424 BPA GRPM)   **Suspense**   (414/424 & 191/391
                                                                         (191/391 BPA GRPM)   BPA GRRZ)

Name (please print)

Address   Apt. #

City   State/Province   Zip/Postal Code

Email: Please check this box ☐ if you would like to receive newsletters and promotional emails from Harlequin Enterprises ULC and its affiliates. You can unsubscribe anytime.

Mail to the Harlequin Reader Service:
IN U.S.A.: P.O. Box 1341, Buffalo, NY 14240-8531
IN CANADA: P.O. Box 603, Fort Erie, Ontario L2A 5X3

Want to try 2 free books from another series? Call 1-800-873-8635 or visit www.ReaderService.com.
